BOA
EDITIONS LTD

The Complete Writings of Art Smith, The Bird Boy of Fort Wayne,
Edited by Michael Martone

the COMPLETE WRITINGS OF
Art Smith
THE BIRD BOY OF FORT WAYNE
Edited by Michael Martone

Michael Martone

Illustrations by Brian Oliu

AMERICAN READER SERIES, No. 35

BOA EDITIONS, LTD. ❧ ROCHESTER, NY ❦ 2020

First Edition
20 21 22 23 7 6 5 4 3 2 1

For information about permission to reuse any material from this book, please contact The Permissions Company at www.permissionscompany.com or e-mail permdude@gmail.com.

Publications by BOA Editions, Ltd.—a not-for-profit corporation under section 501 (c) (3) of the United States Internal Revenue Code—are made possible with funds from a variety of sources, including public funds from the Literature Program of the National Endowment for the Arts; the New York State Council on the Arts, a state agency; and the County of Monroe, NY. Private funding sources include the Max and Marian Farash Charitable Foundation; the Mary S. Mulligan Charitable Trust; the Rochester Area Community Foundation; the Ames-Amzalak Memorial Trust in memory of Henry Ames, Semon Amzalak, and Dan Amzalak; the LGBT Fund of Greater Rochester; and contributions from many individuals nationwide. See Colophon on page 224 for special individual acknowledgments.

Cover Design: Sandy Knight
Interior Design and Composition: Richard Foerster
BOA Logo: Mirko

BOA Editions books are available electronically through BookShare, an online distributor offering Large-Print, Braille, Multimedia Audio Book, and Dyslexic formats, as well as through e-readers that feature text to speech capabilities.

Library of Congress Cataloging-in-Publication Data

Names: Martone, Michael, author. | Smith, Art, 1890-1926. | Oliu, Brian, illustrator.
Title: The complete writings of Art Smith, the Bird Boy of Fort Wayne / edited by Michael Martone ; [historical commentary and biographical information by] Michael Martone ; illustrations by Brian Oliu.
Description: First edition. | Rochester, NY : BOA Editions, Ltd., 2020. | Series: American reader series ; no. 35 | Includes fictional pictures of skywritings with accounts based on events in Smith's life. | Summary: "Fictitious biographical snippets that celebrate the sky-written words of early aviation and the life of the man behind them"— Provided by publisher.
Identifiers: LCCN 2020020152 (print) | LCCN 2020020153 (ebook) | ISBN 9781950774210 (paperback) | ISBN 9781950774227 (ebook)
Subjects: LCSH: Smith, Art, 1890-1926—Anecdotes. | Air pilots—United States—Biography. | Aeronautics—United States—History—20th century—Sources. | Skywriting—Pictorial works.
Classification: LCC TL540.S6 M37 2020 (print) | LCC TL540.S6 (ebook) | DDC 629.13092—dc23
LC record available at https://lccn.loc.gov/2020020152
LC ebook record available at https://lccn.loc.gov/2020020153

BOA Editions, Ltd.
250 North Goodman Street, Suite 306
Rochester, NY 14607
www.boaeditions.org
A. Poulin, Jr., Founder (1938–1996)

For
Lynn Cullen, B.J. Hollars, Deborah Kennedy, Megan Paonessa:
Birds of a Feather

Contents

Some Early Ephemera
Postcards with Captions, Undated
Photography with Notes

Thought to be the only surviving photograph (photographer unknown) of the first "skywriting," the word "CLOUD" appeared in the blue cloudless sky above Fort Wayne, Indiana, on the morning of 3 April 1911. The caption on the reverse reads: "Concocted by aviation pioneer and Fort Wayne native, Art 'The Bird Boy' Smith (seen here as the period, there, dotting the terminal D) and deployed in his home-built aeroplane, its engine barely audible, the artificial cloudlike cloud remaining decipherable for upwards of a minute before it dissipated, dispersed by the high altitude zephyr."

Fort Wayne, Indiana.

A limited edition of this hand-tinted postal card was commissioned to commemorate Art Smith's inaugural airmail flight between his home city of Fort Wayne, Indiana, and the terminus at Toledo, Ohio. The photograph depicts Smith's signature "skywriting" technique there aloft above his hometown, apparently misspelling the name of his former wife, "Aimme." Smith insisted that the smoke should be read as a motto for the new communication enterprise, mainly, "Aim Me!" Though rare, examples of this postcard may be found with the airmail stamp hand-canceled by the Postmaster of Fort Wayne himself, Harry Baals.

Art "The Bird Boy" Smith

The caption on the reverse of this photograph reads: "Photographed over Lake Wawasee near Syracuse, Indiana, on a summer's sunset in 1916, this 'skywriting' was accomplished by the originator of the technique and, at the time, its sole practitioner, Art Smith, The Bird Boy of Fort Wayne. It was said that the smoke generating apparatus for the stunt is attached to the frame of Smith's homemade aeroplane and manipulated by one's feet. This particular manifestation serves as both artifact and its artist's signature. The smoke is said to be harmless, benign as the vapors that arise each dusk from the lake below."

Art "The Bird Boy" Smith

Art Smith, The Bird Boy of Fort Wayne, and the inventor of "skywriting" is captured (in this undated photograph) in the midst of transcribing the final letter of the word "LOOK" to the azure firmament over Ohio, when interrupted by a flight of migrating Canada geese. Notes handwritten on the reverse read: "Captain Art Smith, a veteran of the Great War, reported he took evasive maneuvers when startled by the determined and fast-moving flock in formation, avoiding what would have been certain disaster in the vicinity of Van Wert."

In this series of anonymous photographs, Art "The Bird Boy" Smith is shown attempting to "skywrite" (an aerial technique he recently invented that manufactures a visible vapor affixed in the air in order that it may then be shaped into messages readable from the ground) the name of his future fiancée, Aimee Cour, also of Fort Wayne, Indiana, in the hope of accomplishing the first proposal of marriage of this kind. Unfortunately, it appears, the winds aloft consistently foil his romantic intentions.

Panama

In July of 1915, Art Smith, The Bird Boy of Fort Wayne, became an over-night sensation at the Panama-Pacific International Exposition at San Francisco. He performed acrobatic demonstrations several times each day and closed the fair every night with a pyrophoric display generated by flares attached to the wings of his airplane, their flames tracing the spiraling descent of his falling leaf maneuver through clouds of aerial fireworks. The exposition was timed to celebrate the opening of the Panama Canal, but the city also wished to showcase its recovery from the devastating earthquake of 1906. His celebrity brokered many meetings with visiting dignitaries who witnessed his flying, including Buffalo Bill Cody who gave the young pilot a nugget of gold made into a stick pin and the former Presidents Howard Taft and Theodore Roosevelt, who consented to a short ride in Smith's biplane over the Marina District. Upon landing, The Bird Boy of Fort Wayne and the Bull Moose spoke privately of the Great White Fleet, the Yellow Fever in Panama, and the use of aircraft in war. Smith and the former President had flown over the *USS Birmingham*, at anchor in the bay. Earlier in the year, the cruis-er had carried the commissioners of the Panama-Pacific International

Exposition to the canal and back, but it was also distinguished as the ship that had first launched an airplane, a Curtiss Model D, five years before. Art Smith and the former President circled the famous ship several times, unable to converse in the roar of the engine, but they agreed, after they landed, how vulnerable it all seemed from above.

Also at anchor in San Francisco Bay that day was the armored cruiser *USS Pittsburgh* newly arrived from patrol of the eastern Pacific, scouting, in cooperation with the British, in an effort to deter hostile German raiders. Art Smith would have known the recently rechristened ship, originally named the *USS Pennsylvania*, was also connected to Eugene Ely, the pilot who first launched a shipboard airplane. Two months after the excursion in Norfolk where Ely took off from the foredeck of the *USS Birmingham*, he completed the circuit by landing on the afterdeck of the *USS Pennsylvania* at anchor in the same San Francisco Bay in January of 1911, the first shipboard recovery of an airplane. The feat was accomplished by means of a hook apparatus connected to the tail of his Curtiss Pusher aircraft that captured a cable tethered to the deck. Several months later, in October, during an exhibition in Macon, Georgia, Ely would be killed when he failed to pull out of a dive and crashed. He leapt from the wreckage, seemingly another miraculous survival, only to die seconds later, his spine severed. Art Smith, The Bird Boy of Fort Wayne, was often enmeshed in his own thoughts of wires and wiring. He thought of wires and cables as he rigged the struts and frets of his own home-built airships, turning the turnbuckles and hauling blocks and tackles, and threading the dead-eyes, drawing tight or lightening the load on all the wires and cables threading through the craft, feeling for the tolerances, weaving the wings together, webs of tension and torque, to the point they would snap or sag with slack. "Tuning the rig," you called it. You tuned, tuning the airplane's wires like the strings of a musical instrument so that, in the right air, at the perfect wind speed, the ship would sing, riding the harmonic of a glide, a vibrato in a stall. He thought of his own wiring, how the thought of his thought thinking about thinking ran up and down in the beam of his own flesh fuselage, how nervously his nerves transmitted the tiny calibrations he was constantly making as he considered pitch, roll, and yaw. He is flying. Flying. Until. Like that, a snap. And then he is not. Below him now, the City by the Bay, San Francisco, which was hosting the Panama-Pacific International Exposition to celebrate the opening of the Canal, yes, but to also boast upon the city's recovery after the earthquake and fire in 1906. From above it was easy to see the scars still of the wreckage and the progress of the rebuilding, the grid spread anew on the fill and the altered hills. Easy to see too from there overhead the fault running like a wire up the peninsula. No, more like an incision, a backbone filleted from the folds of meat in the rumbled hills and valleys. He thought again as he climbed of Eugene Ely who stepped out of the wreckage of his plane, thinking, thinking he had survived only to be already dead.

Art Smith, The Bird Boy of Fort Wayne, would often use the still visible ruins of the old Wabash & Erie Canal to navigate a flight through the heart of his home state of Indiana. As he dipped and banked his craft on its southwesterly trajectory, he'd visually leapfrog from the one flash of light to the next flash, sunlight reflecting up from the stagnant waters of the various reservoirs and holding ponds, feeder lines and troughs of the actual boat basins, a necklace of spilled pearls on the green breast of the old prairie. Fort Wayne, his home, was also known as the Summit City (still is) as it occupies the highest elevation on the now derelict waterway running from Toledo on Lake Erie to the north and then to Evansville on the Wabash and the Ohio Rivers to the south. Fort Wayne is situated at the summit of a continental divide. Not as grand as the one further west, this divide separates the watersheds of the Atlantic and the Gulf of Mexico. The strategic location guarded the ancient portage between the two, necessitating all the forts built there before the railroads, turnpikes, and, now, highways. Art Smith would be invited home to circle the city as it celebrated, long after the infrastructure's demise, Canal Days in Fort Wayne, mapping overhead the letters A C A N A L above the confluence of the Saint Joseph and Saint Mary Rivers, the headwaters of the Maumee. The bed of the old canal was the right of way for the Nickel Plate Road and the smoke from its numerous engines always seemed to wash out the day's lofty calligraphy as it rose up from the grid of streets below. The canal as it grew bankrupt and obsolete sparked many "Reservoir Wars," where local residents, plagued now by clouds of mosquitoes emanating from the abandoned and stagnating waters of the canal's remnants, cut the dikes and dams, draining away what was left of the water. After the skywriting, Art Smith would continue the exhibition, diving down into the city, skimming through its streets just above its buildings and tallest trees, enthralling the earthbound crowd celebrating the rapid evolution of transportation, transported, even while fixed at that one spot, by the ease in which Art Smith, their Bird Boy, disappeared, like that, in this new coursing contraption, beyond their imagining.

Art Smith, years later, was in New York City skywriting. Hired by the Dobbs Hat Company of Fifth Avenue to advertise that fall's Felt Hat Day, the date on which men switch from their summer weight straws to the felts and furs of fall. For many years prior, the city's haberdashers and hatters had hired boys to go about the streets on September 15th knocking the straw hats from the heads of neglectful men and crushing them with their feet. Dobbs commissioned a reminder that the time drew near.

HAT DAY and DOBBS

graced the city's skies that September of 1922, the year of the Great Straw Hat Day Riot. The advertisement posted a few days before the date, September 15th, might have confused the pranksters who began destroying hats on the 13th instead and were met with resistance initially by factory workers near Mulberry Bend in Manhattan. The brawl continued for days. Art Smith had no way of knowing this would be in the future when, seven years before, he flew the former President, Theodore Roosevelt, over the gleaming new grounds of the Panama-Pacific

International Exposition in San Francisco. The President had left his chinstrapless hat on the ground that day, the Panama Straw made famous by Roosevelt when he was photographed in another machine, this time a steam shovel, excavating a canal lock in Panama. The picture inspired the adoption of the new style hat, displacing the traditional boater and giving it the name of the place, Panama, even though the hat was made (and still is) in Ecuador. Neither the pilot nor passenger could that day foresee also that Roosevelt's son, Quentin, a pursuit pilot in the 95th Aero Squadron, would be shot down over France on Bastille Day, 1918, his grave marked by a basswood cross fashioned by the Germans from the struts of Lieutenant Roosevelt's Nieuport. Upon hearing that news, Art Smith would remember the flight he took with Quentin's father, the former President, and try to recall if he had ever met the young aviator when he was in training and when Smith was instructing. It was un-likely. Quentin's 95th Squadron's insignia pictured a Kicking Mule. Not the 94th, they sported the more famous insignia of The-Hat-in-the-Ring whose SPADs Smith remembered. Flying low over the landing field of the exposition, Art Smith used the former President's Panama as a kind of target, a beacon, his aid in navigating the space, the field lined by throngs of fairgoers all furiously waving their various styles of hats at the aeroplane as it sped back and forth above them.

My research indicates that there is a consensus about who first conceived of the famous palindrome—A Man. A Plan. A Canal. Panama. Leigh Mercer published the sequence in the November 13, 1948 *Notes & Queries*. Since then, others—Guy Jacobson is suggested—have added words—a cat, a ham, a yak, a yam, a hat—to the middle, extending the word play further after the original. Another Guy, Guy Steele, brought the total up to 49 words. And in 1984, Dan Hoey programed a computer to generate a 540-word palindrome anchored by the original. Still, 1948 seems late for the original invention. Puzzle Masters point out that the original palindrome almost writes itself and that there was a veritable renaissance of word games flourishing in America during the period of the opening of the Panama Canal in 1915. The annotations attached to the several feet of celluloid film, a frame of which is shown here, indicate only that Art Smith, The Bird Boy of Fort Wayne, flying a Vought VE-7, created, the notes insist, this barely legible message over the Chesapeake & Delaware Canal on the occasion of the canal's purchase by the federal government and its incorporation into the new "Intra-Coastal Waterway." It must have been, I imagine, the most difficult skywriting the aviator ever attempted, not merely for its length and duration (it is remarkable that the individual letters remained intact for so long) but also for keeping in mind the oscillating sequence of the composition, its repetitions and symmetries. From the earliest instance of flight and flying, the pilots' experience was marked not by distance traveled, but time in the air, the hours aloft. Airplanes, it seems, were always time machines, suspending not just gravity, but sequence itself. The loops and rolls then were not just a creation in three dimensions, but also even this fourth one. In the air there was or could be—even as there was economic pressure to make flight a trip, a journey, a vector—no beginning, middle, or end. It is an illusion, perhaps, to be able to go back and forth through Time. But isn't it about this time that theories of relativity are being hatched and the elasticity of something so vigorously linear and real as Time was being tested by metaphoric trains and the many phases and shifts one perceives of the experience? And later still, Time itself stalls and stutters, demonstrated by clocks recording two distinct measurements of intervals taken by airplanes circling in opposite directions around and around the globe. The film footage here would have been recorded only a few years before Art Smith would crash in the Ohio farmyard. And yet here these ghostly letters are constructed in such a way as to allow light falling through the frames to reignite, moment after moment, the moment in the past of that past, his past, animating the inanimate, and by reversing the film's direction, back and forth, erase or reconstruct the letters as they bloom and wilt there above the tidal estuary.

Hell

After the Great War, Art Smith, The Bird Boy of Fort Wayne, remained in the United States Army Air Service as a test pilot flying the experimental craft first imagined during the recently concluded hostilities and now realized in Ohio. One such vehicle was a quadrotor named the de Bothezat Helicopter but known to the flight crews at Dayton's McCook Field, as "The Flying Octopus." As its nomenclature implied, the airframe supported four six-bladed rotors, that provided the lift, deployed on sweeping arms of cantilevered girders reinforced by a system of guy wires and turnbuckle stays. In flight, the helicopter very much resembled a roofed railroad truss bridge dislodged by a tornado. Maneuvering was achieved through another twin set of vertical props that the designer George de Bothezat named "steerable airscrews." Two more fans mounted above the underpowered Le Rhone engine (soon to be replaced by a Bentley in a rotary configuration) were meant to provide additional airflow and cool the power plant.

Art Smith was one of only two men, the other being Major T. H. Bane, qualified to take the contraption aloft. The controls and instruments were particularly complicated. The aircraft mounted dual spoked wheels for banking, a yoke for the whole aircraft's pitch and trim which was wired with six toggles to adjust each rotor's variable pitch setting, a half dozen throttles, one regulated with one's knees, and a set of foot pedals for yaw. The flap-like air brakes were engaged via an umbilical belt attached to the pilot's waist and activated with a rotary motion of his hips during the landing. Though the airplane itself was scrapped in 1924, the control array is on display at the Smithsonian Institution.

Surprisingly, the airplane flew. Or more accurately, on 18 December 1922, the helicopter hovered two meters above the ground. The contraption proved to be a remarkably stable platform, due, perhaps, to its many angled lift rotors canted toward the center of gravity. In its year of testing, the craft successfully lifted off over one hundred times, eventually attaining a sustained altitude above twenty meters, and was able to carry up to four passengers to that height.

The early test flights demonstrated the craft's ability to do little more than vertical takeoff and landing. Its lateral motion was dictated by the prevailing wind that would push the craft hither and yon in an uncontrolled fashion. Art Smith, in later flights, attempted to address the craft's directional deficiency, going so far as to attach his skywriting mechanism with its panel of instruments to map the vectoring he sought to achieve. Pictured here, the result of his experimentation that fall, are the unstable remnants of erratic and abrupt course correction. An abandoned "HELICOPTER," perhaps, or an aborted "HELLO" graced the sky over Dayton for a moment as the Octopus, generating fog from all of its many spans and booms, left a telltale tracing of its seemingly stable and steady and sustained flight.

The Ampersand

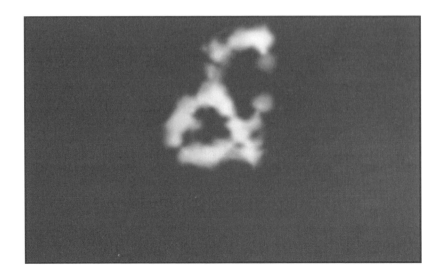

In 1916, in the air over his native city, Art Smith, The Bird Boy of Fort Wayne, attempted to skywrite an ampersand in support of Democratic President Woodrow Wilson's election to a second term. In creating the symbol, Smith wrote later, he also wanted to persuade the President and Congress to take America into the Great War, allied with Great Britain and France, where the use of the airplane in aerial combat had commenced and expanded in thrilling new tactics and aerobatics. Smith believed that the ampersand's tracing replicated the tortured maneuverings of airplanes while "dogfighting" in the skies over Europe. It was only later, upon reflection, Art Smith saw, in its curlicues and crossovers, that the smoke-generated ampersand over Fort Wayne outlined, in a swift gesture, the character of a proudly perched bird. This insight spurred him to adopt the logogram as his personal symbol and to commission its pattern on several devices of jewelry and to have it embroidered as his insignia upon his flying attire and upon the flanks of the fuselages of his future flying machines.

Benday

In early September of 1916 while recovering in Indiana from the surgery on his broken leg, the injury he sustained in the crash at Sapporo ending his first tour of Japan, Art Smith, The Bird Boy of Fort Wayne, received word that Benjamin Henry Day, Jr. had died in Summit, New Jersey. Smith was introduced to Day, the son of the founder of the *New York Sun*, five years before when Smith was engaged by the editor of the Hillsdale, Michigan, newspaper, *The Hillsdale Daily Standard Herald*, to deliver the paper to the nearby towns of Camden, Jonesville, Litchfield, Pittsford, and Reading. While not writing any words in the sky, Art instead dropped words upon the towns, the newspapers bundled with jute hay baling twine. He circled as the bundle descended, waiting as the recipients below gathered up the packages and waved to him in gratitude. The arrangement anticipated the more complicated logistics the United States Post Office would soon inaugurate for delivering its mail and in whose service Art Smith would give his life a decade hence. Occasionally, while making such deliveries for the *Daily Standard Herald*, Art Smith would spill his cargo over acres of Michigan, the knots in the twine giving way and a squall of newspaper broadsheets raining down upon the citizens below.

There was nothing to be done as the unbound sheaves shifted and spun to the ground. Aloft, Art Smith, conscious that the prop wash of his plane stirred further the thermal meanderings of his spilled cargo, delighted in the notion that all these letters were like motes of dust descending. And though the scored pages flapped like birds, they did not fly or soar but covered the countryside below in shoals and drifts in the open fields and along the fencerows. He watched from above while those below gleaned the litter from the landscape. It was like following the bouncing ball in the new movie cartoon sing-alongs. He had seen one recently animating the song "Come Josephine in My Flying Machine." Art drifted away from the chaotic commotion below, his memory drifting too. He had met Josephine Magner, the song's romantic subject, who also performed on the demonstration circuit, parachuting from dirigibles, the blooming silk of her bobbing chute, another oscillating orb through the air...

But we have drifted ourselves here. This entry was to annotate the elliptical pattern Art Smith, The Bird Boy of Fort Wayne, produced over Summit, New Jersey, in the fall of 1916, out of respect for the recently deceased Ben Day. Ben Day invented the printing process that bears his name, *benday*, composed of fields of equally sized and distributed dots of ink that created, when arrayed on newsprint, the illusion of depth on flat photos and allowed for the expansion of color in the Sunday funnies of the nation's newspapers. The sky that day was cloudless, a perfect canvas for his skywriting. To replicate and apply the benday's precise rigorous pattern Art Smith summoned all his powers and skills of aviation. The break healing in his aching bone was being painfully knitted back together. Through the throbbing pain, he bore down hard on his plane's rudder. Afterwards as he flew above the field of clouds he had created, he looked earthward and through the stippled screen of rings, marveling at the illusion of depth, the disruption of space, the perforation of the sky the stencil of dots brought about, the dappled nature of the dimpled shadows cast upon the ground below. The *Oh! Oh!*

Oh! Oh...! He found himself repeating as the sieve of smoke imprinted itself upon his memory and, bit by bit, a dot at a time, upon this empty photographic plate now exposed to this one moment's moment.

A Father's Vision

In 1911, Art Smith, The Bird Boy of Fort Wayne, created, with his new skywriting apparatus, this letter E over Driving Park (later to be renamed Memorial Park, the site of Smith's own memorial after his fatal crash in 1926) during a celebratory exhibition of his flying skills concluding his first successful tour of the Midwest. Only days before, in Beresford, South Dakota, his prowess in his home-built craft had garnered him $750, enough money for Smith to take a Pullman sleeper home to Fort Wayne. There was more than enough left over to schedule an appointment with the world famous oculist in Chicago. Art Smith's father, James, had been, for years, going blind, and Art had promised him a visit to the highly regarded specialist in hopes of slowing, if not reversing, his father's degenerating vision the moment after his flying provided sufficient funds to do so. And now that time had come. But first, Art Smith led his father out into the meadow of Driving Park and invited him to lie down and gaze with clouded eyes upon the cloudless skies over Fort Wayne. The crowd that had gathered to witness the full program of aerial acrobatics Smith demonstrated now also gazed aloft as the bold letter took shape overhead. Mr. Smith, supine, when asked by a reporter from *The Journal Gazette*

if he could read the writing in the sky that his son in his distant flying machine was still laboring to complete replied, "No. No. It is all blank, empty, a sheet of white paper."

The crowd gathered that day on the east side of Fort Wayne easily saw the panoramic E, recognized instantly the initial letter of visual acuity floating above them in the way it was also suspended, gigantic, over the tapering column of other declining letters (C, D, F, L, N, O, P, T, Z) found upon the eye charts in the offices of their own, less famous, oculists of the city. The Dutch ophthalmologist, Hermann Snellen, devised his optotypes in 1862 and eye care professionals stateside had long utilized his charts. Art Smith, The Bird Boy of Fort Wayne, continued his patient calligraphy. His father, spread-eagle on the grassy floor of the park, fixed his apparently unfixable eyes upon the blank slate of sky over his head. His son would say later that he believed his father's condition was brought on by the sun's incessant glare, his father working out-of-doors as a carpenter's assistant, his vision screwed down to mark the fine guide lines of the sawing. Perhaps the oculist in Chicago would suggest some kind of exercises for the eye. Art Smith imagined performing complicated feats of aerial dexterity, inscribing cursive trails of smoke that his father would follow from below, strengthening the subtle optic muscles' ability to track, the lenses to focus and magnify, to shutter and flood the retinal nerve with informative light. The crowd gathered that day grew fatigued with the seeing, craning their necks to see through the tidal sheets of light. Now, in the corners of their eyes, shadows, perhaps after-images of their staring, appeared. A flock of turkey buzzards, *Cathartes aura*, circled, circling above them, homing in on the invisible scent of something dying or dead nearby. The citizens of Fort Wayne as they stared at the drifting black birds, floating punctuation to the now new second and even larger letter that eclipsed the disappearing original E, shielded their eyes against the sun.

The third letter appeared to stretch for miles in all directions, curving gently at its far reaches, the fluid vapor seemingly draining over the horizons. Art Smith's father remained stretched out upon the lawn of Driving Park continuing to report, "Nothing. Nothing. Nothing." And again, "Nothing." The crowd gathered there (*The Journal Gazette* had estimated several hundred) now joined the elder Smith on the ground, dropping down in groups of threes or fours, families, clubs, whole curious church congregations. They were weary from the sustained awkward wrenching of their necks from the hours of watching Art zoom back and forth over their heads, composing the expanding E's one after the other. The field was blanketed with bodies, arrayed like patches on a crazy quilt. Those sighted could see clearly, of course, the long seemingly endless strokes of the letters' various linear runs. It appeared almost like the sky above them was being plowed, turned over to reveal furrows of clouds. Or perhaps the sky itself seemed to be imprisoned, barred behind the paralleling matrix, a confinement of space captured in smaller squares of space. The sun set beyond the city to the west. And as their collective eyes followed the blooming line heading in that direction, caught there too in the joint peripheral vision of the masses, a clutch of subtle sun dogs flared up, north and south, lodged in the teary corners of thousands of eyes. The optic phenomenon parenthetically haloed the light with more light. These spectaculars were lost, of course, on the blind eyes of Art Smith's father who, the next day, left with his son for the appointment in Chicago there to meet with the world famous oculist. In a skyscraper office building within the Loop, the Smiths learned, sadly, there was nothing to be done. Later, the finality of the news sinking in, they, father and son, gazed out the window of their room at The Palmer House, out through the slim fissure between the crowded buildings to the sliver of severely clear sky apparent over Lake Michigan, and both imagined for a moment the brilliant future of Art's life in the opulent and unoccluded air.

A Field Guide to the Birds of Indiana

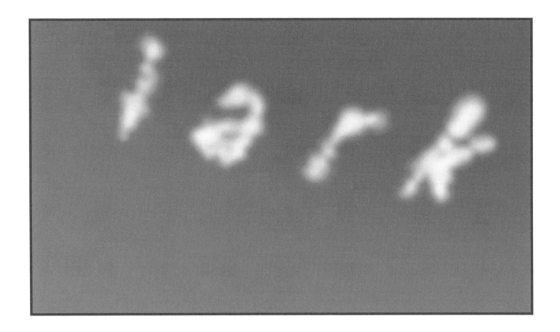

Although there is no way to say for sure that Art Smith, The Bird Boy of Fort Wayne, read much more than the literature provided by the various publishing ventures of the Church of Christ, Scientist, this skywriting (produced with the oily black soot of his initial formulations of smoke) which appeared over the rapidly disappearing Limberlost of Adams and Jay counties in northeastern Indiana, suggests he was familiar with the writings of Gene Stratton-Porter. In order to complete this stunt, he would have flown south from Fort Wayne to circle above the small town of Geneva. This would have been in the fall of 1913 or the spring of 1914. By that time the great 13,000-acre wooded swamp was nearly drained, primordial Lake Engle siphoned off and lowered, leveled into a series of muddy puddles, the forest logged for barrels and shipbuilding. With the vast wetlands vanished, the sky above would have been empty of most native avian species and its migratory fowl diverted further west to the Mississippi Valley flyways. The carrion raptors, however, would have been busy still, scouring the cloudless sky.

Art, The Bird Boy of Fort Wayne, Smith, returned in 1915 to the drained and now cultivated tableland that had once been the Limberlost. The agricultural tiling of the retired swamp was extensive and quite successful, the air that day seems to have been saturated with a thick particulate dust kicked up by the moldboard plowing proceeding below. He would have had ample opportunity to observe the ambitious plotting of township section roads and the platting of the future farm fields that create the telltale signature of Midwestern agriculture. The cardinal, a common bird with extraordinary scarlet plumage and of a species that does not flock, would become the state bird of Indiana in 1933. It would have adapted readily to the now cleared fields studded with the thinned copses of second growth woodlot left to stand, spreading out to the distant hazy horizon. It is thought that this was Art Smith's first attempt to tint a work of skywriting, reflecting, in the opaque fog, the coloring of its vibrant subject.

During the 1933 debate in the legislature that resulted in the election of the cardinal as the state bird an amendment was offered that nominated the firefly as the Indiana state insect. During the summer barnstorming seasons, his performances concluded in the dusk, Art Smith piloted his acrobatic aeroplane low over the flat Indiana farm fields that once had been the bed of a shallow inland sea. Fireflies in the millions, it seemed to him, sparked off of the tasseled tops of the cornstalks. The swarms of flashing insects glimmered as they rose up in pulsing clouds, twisting drafts of strobing light. The leading edges of his craft's canvas wings became coated with the light as he struck through the buggy nebula, the light still throbbing in what seemed to him to be some kind of coded message, a blinkered telegraphy. On the ground, the barns backlit by the sunset, he is said to have loved watching the squadrons of swallows juke through the shadows, jinking in and out of the loft doors, swooping up around the silo, strafing the feathering windmill, stalling, then, executing emergency landings into the muddy nests daubed in evening eaves. All around, fireflies mimicked the distant stuttering heat lightning.

The cleared land attracted great flocks of the invasive subspecies of starling. Returning from Indianapolis, flying north over the vast open expanse between Geneva and Berne, Art Smith startled one such flock with the persistent buzz of his new Lawrance J-1 engine. The birds rose up from the gleaned fields below in one great roiling scarf, the massive murmuration wrapping around his craft and then billowing away from it only to react and regroup to form a trailing banner replicating the exhausted compositions of Smith's own cloudy skywriting, but now in a much more fluid cursive style that, then, blotted, ran, and smeared before stretching out into a sublime serif scattering of contorted and convulsive alphabets. In that cloud of agitated blackbirds, he answered, writing back in the patient deliberate block printing that the meandering school of birds, in its frenzy, disturbed, stirred up, and ultimately erased, draining the salutation down into a series of mesmerizing vortices.

In 1924, the year of Gene Stratton-Porter's death in Los Angles, her limousine demolished by a streetcar, Art Smith ventured to Rome City, Indiana, to affix this message above the pristine Sylvan Lake. Stratton-Porter's second cabin, known as Wildflower Woods, stands on the shore of the lake. She wrote a dozen novels including *Freckles* and *A Girl of the Limberlost*. Making a silent film version of the Limberlost books brought her to California and to her untimely demise. *Wings* was her last nature book published when she was alive. Her natural histories of the vanished wetlands of Indiana contain extensive inventories of the dispersed and the devastated flora and fauna of the region. She avidly spoke out against predatory millinery practices and refused to wear a hat. Her photographs of various birds in flight are thought to be the first such exposures taken from the vantage of an airplane. There is no evidence that Art Smith had ever met Gene Stratton-Porter or read any of her many books even though the number in print is thought to be in excess of 50 million. Perhaps there is nothing more to it but that it was spring when this affixation appeared over Noble County, the time when the solidary red-breasted robin, a thrush, separates itself from the northward bearing migratory flocks to establish breeding territories it defends vigorously with its beautifully melodious and memorable song.

Mom

In 1925, flying over North Highlands, with his mother, Ida, on board, Art Smith, The Bird Boy of Fort Wayne, negotiated a crash landing after the motor driving his de Havilland choked. Descending from two thousand feet, he expertly voplaned his craft to earth. Neither was injured. It was the second such emergency landing he survived with his mother who later said: "I looked at Art and touched his shoulder. When he smiled at me, I knew I was with my boy and I was safe." Days later, his airplane repaired, Smith took to the sky again to commemorate the event. His mother, safely on the ground this time, blew kisses into the air from her gloved hands.

Observed that day from further west, Art Smith's homage to his mother read as an exclamation. A farmer harrowing a field off Bass Road, his attention drawn by the pesky buzz of the airplane overhead, called for his wife to come see as the letters appeared there, punctuated by the blotting clouds. A year later, after the crash he would not survive, Art Smith would be laid to rest at the nearby Lindenwood Cemetery. During the interment there, a flight of de Havilland airships would bomb the gravesite with a dusting of flower petals. Ida, it is said, held up her hand as if to receive a homing pigeon. Or a hawk.

Further Writing

One of Art Smith's earliest aerial attempts pays homage to the inventors of heavier-than-air controlled powered flight. It was composed over the open ocean of North Carolina's Outer Banks near Kill Devil Hills in 1915 after several trial runs spelled out with a stick upon the sand dunes. Back in 1910, Smith had traveled from Fort Wayne to Indianapolis to see the brothers demonstrate their craft. Returning home, an inspired Art Smith breathed out upon the window of the interurban whisking him north and in the fog now clouding the car's glass he spelled out, with a trembling finger, the name of the creators and in so doing prefigured his own invention of the skywriting in the rapidly approaching future.

During the 1916 barnstorming tour of the upper Midwest, Art Smith, The Bird Boy of Fort Wayne, wrote this over the town of Wahpeton, North Dakota. The meaning of the message was unclear. One interpretation has it that Smith was asserting his "right" to land his craft on the one paved municipal street below, the citizens of Wahpeton being notorious for their dislike of the many stunt fliers now crisscrossing the region. The other theory holds that this was a signal to Smith's ground chase crew that he would be turning "right" and heading to the more welcoming town of Breckenridge, Minnesota, on the eastern bank of the northern flowing Red River.

On November 18th, 1925, the Scottish Rite Cathedral opened in Fort Wayne, Indiana. Art Smith flew above the ceremonies, inscribing this message along the corridor of Fairfield Avenue. The Valley of Fort Wayne Ancient and Accepted Order of the Scottish Rite, a growing order of the Masons, sought, at the time, to expand. Max Irmscher & Sons began construction in April of 1924 with 200 masons, mostly local, taking a year and a half to complete the project costing over $1 million. Two steam shovels took six weeks to excavate the ballroom. Over 350,000 bricks were used in the construction, adding to the building's reputation as the most "fire-proof" in the city. Art Smith had longed to be "tapped" by the secret fraternal organization. He often thought of his skywriting as a kind of masonry. The smoke might be like grouting, or the words concocted out of that vapor a signifier of "wall." But his contribution to that glorious occasion proved inconsequential, the writing disappearing almost as soon as it was written, and goes unremarked in the printed commemorative program.

Not long before his untimely death in February of 1926, Art Smith, The Bird Boy of Fort Wayne, affixed the above above an open field straddling the Indiana-Ohio border near Paulding. At the time, Smith served as a pilot for the recently formed Air Service of the United States Post Office flying the routes between New York and Chicago. He would often modify his Curtiss Carrier Pigeon aircraft with his skywriting apparatus, several times advertising over the large metropolitan regions to **Write Home** or **Write Mother** via the PO. It is harder to explain this message affixed over the open and desolate pastureland of western Ohio. Smith left no notes in this regard. Who was the intended audience for this swiftly dissipating and somewhat lyrical missive?

When

The Indianapolis department store,* When, commissioned Art Smith, The Bird Boy of Fort Wayne, to address the sky above the Indianapolis Motor Speedway in May of 1920, the year the famous race instituted the 4 lap qualification test that became known as "time trials," conducted over the several preceding weekends leading up to the 500-mile main event. After applying his craft, Art Smith would circle above the racetrack as the lone automobile completed the timed circuit and the vapor of the original message, exhausted, dissipated. If his fuel allowed, the aviator would commence to reapply the commercial message in the freshening Indiana spring air, tracing the washed-out shadows of the previous attempt.

---

* The promotion was so successful that other Indianapolis department stores hired Art Smith to skywrite over the Circle City. These included Wm. H. Block Co.:

And L. Strauss & Co.:

As well as L. S. Ayres & Co., famously misspelling it:

Correcting it immediately, Smith improvised an impromptu flyby, drafting the dot above the **i** into the long articulated armature of the **Y** in his wake:

The Tragic Elopement

Art Smith, The Bird Boy of Fort Wayne, attempting to elope with his fiancée, Aimee Cour, escaping from Fort Wayne to Hillsdale, Michigan, where he believed they could be married quickly, crashed his home-built biplane, in which they were flying together, tried to land in a field of soft sand south of town that fouled the gear and flipped the machine over short of their destination. Wrapped in bandages from head to foot, they were married days later in a hotel where they were recuperating, there being no hospitals in Hillsdale, both fainting several times during the hastily arranged ceremony. Art recalled later he remembered little of the event as several times the doctors in attendance administered the hypodermic. Art sustained several deep bruises but escaped, his doctors told him, a serious concussion of the brain. Aimee, more acutely injured, convalesced from what was diagnosed as severe back and spinal damage, the pain of which would plague her for the rest of her life. Art, now ambulatory though still being treated for pain, repaired the machine as Aimee rested in her room. Very soon, Aimee heard the sound of its Eldridge engine aloft outside the hotel, the machine itself a mere speck in the blue. Even in his weakened state, Art Smith sought to announce what he often said was the best thing that ever happened to him on God's green earth.

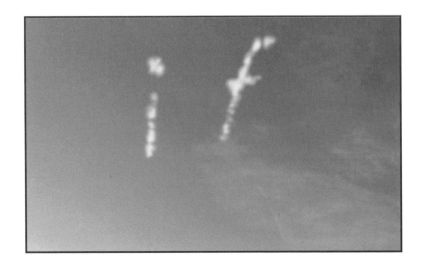

The letters "i" and "f" appeared in the clear blue sky over Fort Wayne, Indiana, during the fall of 1921, inscribed there by Art Smith, The Bird Boy of Fort Wayne, using his patented device to generate the fog for sky-writing. Smith often commented that he wished he could find a way to produce the messages he wrote in the sky instantaneously instead of the slow sequences produced, one after the other, as his machine, flying a kind of aerial ballet, moved from point A to point B through time and space. While Art Smith was able to solve many physical problems presented by the invention of flight, he was unable to overcome the linear constraints seemingly built into the act of writing in this manner. In this case the "i" appeared first in the sky followed then by the "f" creating, with every pitch change and sputter of the engine's report, a kind of suspense suspended above the literate observers down below. And then...

In the summer of 1921, Art Smith, The Bird Boy of Fort Wayne, read for the first time the writings of the mathematician Daniel Bernoulli as he convalesced after his crash into a cornfield near Lima, Ohio. He had been flying and crashing now for more than a dozen years, doing so, as it appeared to him, with only the instinct of the avian species and the tinkerer's knack for having a go, never fully realizing the physical laws of nature that he and other pioneers of flying were employing in, what seemed to be, the miracle of heavier than air powered flight as well as their death-defying stunts and maneuvers. Only a week before writing "lift" above, Art Smith was moved to inscribe the equation

over Lake Wawasee near Syracuse, Indiana, its waters congested by the Labor Day boating populace mystified by the formula floating overhead.

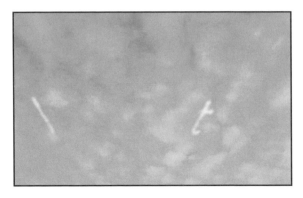

"The duration of space in space" was how Art Smith, The Bird Boy of Fort Wayne, described it, the punctuation of the fading letters accentuating the empty empty distance between those letters that remained temporarily suspended in the cold cold stratosphere. After completing another composition, Art Smith would often cut the power to his noisy engine, and he and his aircraft would descend, gliding earthward on the wings of a welcome silence. A silence composed of the static frequency of the wind flowing over all the surfaces of his body as he waded into the altitudes of denser air and the solid grasp of invisible gravity.

The Unknown

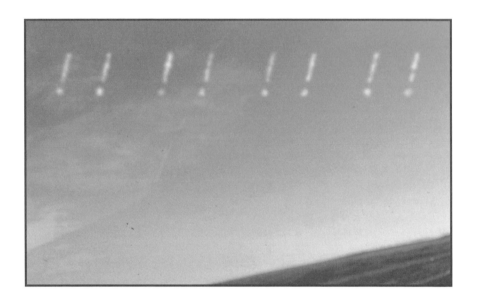

In October of 1921, nearly three years after the Armistice, Art Smith, The Bird Boy of Fort Wayne, sails to France to attend the selection of the American Unknown. On Sunday the 23rd, the ceremony is conducted at the Hotel de Ville in Châlons-sur-Marne with four caskets of unknown American soldiers disinterred from cemeteries at Aisne-Marne, Meuse-Argonne, Somme, and St. Mihiel converging on the city from four different directions. At that moment, Art Smith (flying a borrowed French SPAD VII specially modified to accommodate his aerial writing mechanism) applies the series (shown above) of evocative exclamations marks (designed to commemorate the moment of the cessation of hostilities and punctuate, in relative silence, the solemn proceedings going on below) in the sky over the city of Chalon-sur-Saône in Burgundy, an error (!) as the cities are often confused by those unfamiliar with the many Departments of France.

Chalon-sur-Saône, while not the actual venue for the selection of America's Unknown Soldier, is thought to be the birthplace of photography, and its museum contains the Pyréolophore, the world's first internal combustion engine. Art Smith, aloft, has no way of knowing that this history is preserved below while, he believes, another kind of history is being made. Now, nearly one hundred years after Nicéphore Niépce invented the technology of photography, Art Smith throttles up the Renault V8 powering his SPAD and turns toward Paris where, above the Eiffel Tower, he inscribes this curling cloud captured on film. He does so partly as an homage to Santos-Dumont's feat of 1901, steering his Dirigible #6 around the structure to win the Deutsch Prize, but also as his tribute to the Unknown whose casket, draped in the Stars and Stripes and still sporting the dozen white roses Sergeant Edward Younger used to indicate his selection, is making its way to the capital city by dedicated train.

Captain Fred Zinn, a Michigander, who flew for the French *Aéronautique Militaire* and was the first to successfully deploy photographic combat reconnaissance from an airplane, introduces Art Smith to Gertrude Stein, the American expatriate art collector and author, that fall in Paris during the ceremonies surrounding the Unknown's repatriation. At the writer's atelier, 27 rue de Fleurus, Art Smith admires the walls of paintings he finds hanging there, noting how so many seem so flat to him, swaths of color similar to the way the land appears from the air, scored and divided into fields and pastures by roads and hedges. Captain Zinn then produces several prints of his wartime reconnoitering to confirm Smith's insight, pointing out how the landscape grid had been disrupted by the asymmetry of the trench works, bombardment, and bastions. They talk of the theory of camouflage, of ground and foil, and the heroic convoy of Parisian taxicabs turning the Battle of the Marne. Miss Stein recalls watching the aerial dogfights in the late afternoons, the frenzied brushstrokes of smoke, the fiery streaks of fire. An observation balloon burning, its occupants buoyed by their tethered canopies of silk as they fell earthward.

The disappearance of all birdlife from the *campagne* for seasons after the Armistice. She is, of course, intrigued with Smith's skywriting, and the following day he demonstrates with this display over the Left Bank's *arrondissements*, mapping in the air a woven net of clouds that seem, as the time passes and the exhausted smoke settles toward the ground, to expand and ensnare the whole city in a soft mesh of whitish ash.

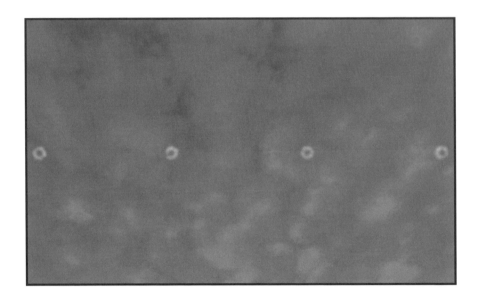

At Le Havre, the cruiser *USS Olympia* departs for America with the casket of the Unknown. Art Smith circles the port in his SPAD, observing the ceremonies proceeding below. The French destroyers beyond the breakwater deliver a precise seventeen-gun salute that the *Olympia*, making way through the harbor, answers with its own salvo. The ship, escorted by a flotilla of torpedo boats, gathers steam. The crowds on the quay below disperse—the bands and battalions of soldiers, the school children and boy scouts, the fire brigade and gendarmerie. Lost in thought, he banks, a hard rudder, coming about one last time heading inland to land at Le Bourget Aerodrome. Behind him would be the Unknown on the voyage home and this periodic trail, like wreaths in the water, crumbs of clouds, an ellipsis, holding open a space, growing smaller in the distance, and falling, always falling, always falling short.

String

Early in 1911, Art Smith, The Bird Boy of Fort Wayne, traveled the Midwest, his aeroplane shipped via rail from venue to venue, on what would become a tour of disasters, a series of malfunctions and crashes in Sterling and Mattoon, Illinois, and in Muncie, Indiana. Most often to blame for the catastrophes were the conditions of the landing fields of the various events. The local sponsors, having never before witnessed heavier-than-air flight, could not begin to imagine the proper conditions for a successful takeoff and landing. They failed to take into consideration and neglected to clear scrub and shrubbery, brush and bush, even whole mature trees obstructing a runway, if one could call it a runway at all, and Art Smith certainly did not. His paltry percentages of the gates at these fiascos barely began to pay for his costly repairs and his spartan accommodations of transportation to the next unscripted debacle.

Little did he know but at the same time in San Francisco a pilot named Eugene Ely successfully landed, for the first time in history, a plane on a ship at sea. His Curtiss pusher aircraft touched down on a teakwood platform built atop the hull of the armored cruiser *USS*

Pennsylvania anchored in the middle of the bay. Hugh Robinson, a circus performer, concocted the apparatus that allowed an aeroplane to be trapped and arrested on such a short landing strip. A long metal hook, deployed from the plane's keel, grappled a cable spread on the deck. The cable ends, threaded through a block and tackle and counterweighted with a carefully calibrated cluster of sandbags, stopped the craft over a few stretched yards. The Navy reported the event with much fanfare, calling it a Controlled Crash.

It was at this time too that Art Smith observed while en route, flying to yet another show, this time in Adrian, Michigan, the optical illusion created by the decreasing density of the air at altitude and the deflection of light in the thinning atmosphere that caused the apparent warping of the earth as one rose up above 4,000 feet. At those giddy heights and perhaps under the influence of several severe concussions, he hallucinated, feeling the physics of flight fall away from him and the band of gravity reassert itself, no longer invisible but there hauling his plane earthward as if on a leash. In the clouds, he said later, he saw a gigantic scaffolding of articulated springs and stays, struts and wires, a massive trapeze of suspended cirrus clouds descending from heaven onto which an aviator could affix, swinging from one vine to the next, a kind of aeronautic brachiation.

Over the years, after he invented the device to "skywrite," Art Smith found as he fell, in a lazy corkscrew spin, that he had fallen into the habit of writing a kind of vertical signature or more accurately a ligature tethering certain descents, coupling the realms through which he navigated. Smoky stair steps, a wispy ladder.

Today, a full-scale replica of Art Smith's early Flyer is displayed, suspended from the ceiling by means of a web of cables above the security checkpoint at the Fort Wayne International Airport. The fidelity of the model's construction is exacting, right down to the greased cotter pins in the landing gear, and the viewer is reminded just how fragile and fraught the early aircraft were, rigged with piano wire and waxed leather stitching. The exacting attention to detail is obvious. There, one can see the baling twine or thongs of rawhide used in the hasty repairs long ago, splinting a strut, splicing a guy line through a grommet. The plane seems to float above the conveyors below, feeding the x-ray machines with the carry-on luggage and the pairs of shoes. If observed closely the aeroplane does seem to sway, the wires flexing, perhaps twisting in some ghost turbulence above the milling crowds waiting to board their own flights to somewhere else.

For hours, Art Smith, The Bird Boy of Fort Wayne, in his capacity as a test pilot, circled Langley Field in a modified DH-4 daylight bomber. Reading over and over from a list of single syllable words into a radio microphone, he transmitted the signal to the receiving ground station below. The antenna, a 100-foot length of wire made of fine phosphor-bronze strands, like gossamer, weighing just an ounce and a half, had been spooled out beyond the tail upon takeoff. The experiment was to ascertain what words would broadcast well from aloft. He repeated, "Maim, maim, main, main, make, make, man, man, map, map, mar, mar, mask, mask, match, match, mate, mate, maul, maul, maze, maze, mean, mean…" Smith did not have a receiver. The engine's roar and the wind swaddling the open cockpit made hearing anything in return impossible. In the static between the words' echoing, both the small sizzle produced by the radio and the larger ambient howling swirling around him, he pictured the injection of his stuttering speech into the invisible stream of the space between space. Of course, he had no way of knowing then of electromagnetic troughs and waves, that his broadcast was and would become a component of the leading edge of that initial radio pulse, pulsing still and still expanding outward into the greater galaxy. No, lulled by his recited litany, he imagined something more along the lines of a leaf falling, switching back and forth on some unseen current, still a creature connected to gravity, as he was, and not flying off weightlessly, in all directions, out into empty space.

In April of 1925, Art Smith returned home to Fort Wayne, contracted to advertise the new commercial radio station, WOWO, broadcasting then on 1320 kHz. Chester Keen who also owned the Main Auto Supply Company owned the station, and Smith was paid for the job with parts he would use to customize his airmail Curtiss and his own aeroplane. He employed as an orientating landmark the downtown intersections of the city's rail lines where the yards of the Pennsylvania and Wabash meshed. There, Smith stitched together the call letters, the double-ues' undulations mimicking the amplitude of radio waves. Below him, he could see the many steam engines shunting back and forth on the tracks, making their own visible smoke and steam, more telegraphic than sonic, the dots and dashes blooming along the lines as if their semaphoring was a kind of response to his own. But silent, all of this in silence, as his altitude and the constant crash of wind muted the reports of the whistles blowing when the engines picked up speed or changed directions. Seeing the bursts of smoke below him, Art Smith summoned up that sound—that familiar wail of it, its panting exhaustion, its depressed minor key, that accumulating and crashing of the sound, wave after wave after wave.

Scale

From the air, the world, falling away below, grew so small. It always struck Art Smith, The Bird Boy of Fort Wayne, how diminished, how minuscule the people in the crowds of people who had come to see him fly became as he climbed. They shrank. Or, more exactly—collapsed, flattened, contracted. Even evaporated. Boiled down to nothing. He was aware of this and other optical illusions flying created. The forced perspective of this new kind of distance was proof that human eyes were not built to see clearly under such circumstances. Our eyes were not like those of the raptors, who could glimpse and target the smallest of the small growing smaller as they soared.

This effect never failed to amaze his passengers back in the early days of exhibition flying. Those observers would have been lucky to have climbed as high as the rooftop of a five-story building or the belfry of a church steeple. They squealed through the prop wash and roar of the engine, "Look, look!" their shouts scrambled and shushed. They gestured instead, squeezing the air between their closing fingers to pinch upon the ever-compressing image of a shrinking spectator below.

Art Smith had met Paul Guillow, a naval aviator, during The Great War, when together with other test pilots and instructors they developed the close comradeship of the airmen's barracks in Ohio. This intense friendship went so far as to the creation of a tontine whose capital consisted of patent applications, blueprints, and aeronautical drawings of wing, engine, and fuselage design each individual club member had devised. Guillow imagined after the war that there would be a public interest in scale models of the life-sized aeroplanes he and his compatriots had built in barns and backyard sheds at the dawn of powered flight. Far from the war where the exigencies of combat were accelerating design modifications of the new fighter aircraft at the front, Art Smith and Paul Guillow experimented with the miniaturization of aeroplanes from the past, fabricating from balsa wood, tissue paper, dope, thread gauge wire and foil, the replicas of their flying machines.

The war over, Paul Guillow went on to found the company that to this day bears his name. Guillow manufactures model kits of actual aircraft as well as simple penny gliders that when thrown with their pliant wooden wings warped to the proper degree perform rudimentary aeronautic maneuvers, barrel rolls and loops, as they sail through the air. Guillow engaged his former barracks mate and fellow tontine subscriber, Art Smith, to compose, in skywriting, advertising for the new company. Above Wakefield, Massachusetts, in 1925, Art Smith experimented, constructing the message, scaled scales, careful to retrace the schematic he had drawn, **s c a l e,** on a piece of gridded paper onto an unruled sky. From the ground, his airplane was but a mere speck in the heavens, a pinpoint, the nib of an invisible pen from which the letters billowed forth and then disappeared in an invented distance.

After all these years of "skywriting" it was still difficult for Art Smith to judge how his compositions appeared to the earthbound onlooker. From where he sat, he was lost in a maze of his own invention. He counted out the seconds during the long reach of an "l," to the point where he felt the stroke should be stopped. The curves and arches and loops were more difficult to produce. He must hold a banking turn while monitoring his compass as it swung through the wide arch of bearings. In the midst of a witty sentiment, he was entangled and enveloped by the clouds, the fog, he himself had generated.

Your eyes can play tricks on you. They seem not to be calibrated to see, to comprehend size over great distance, a perspective now made readily possible by heavier-than-air powered flight. Art Smith would, the next year, mistake a light in a farmyard for the lights of the landing strip in Toledo. One night, he found in the depths of one pocket of his flight jacket a newly minted dime whose obverse bore the profile of Liberty in a winged cap though widely mistaken as portraiture of Mercury, the messenger god. He drew it out, and, out of his pocket, the dime's silvered surface caught a flash of moonlight. That clear night, flying with the full moon riding on his wing tip, Smith eyed the planetary heft of that moon muscling into the sky and then, like that, he held up the coin, the thin little wafer tweezed between his fingers, held it at arm's length, and saw it blot out any inkling of another nearby world in all that nearby closing darkness.

Word Cross

In Nara, Art Smith, The Bird Boy of Fort Wayne, was introduced to avia-trix Katherine Stinson, The Flying School Girl, by General Nagaoka, the imperial impresario who had organized the visits, when their separate demonstration tours of Japan intersected in the soggy city south and west of Tokyo. The citizens of Nara had built a temporary open-sided hangar where the pilots and their aeroplanes took shelter during a steady downpour. Smith returned to Japan with the 1915 model biplane he flew during his first visit. He was very interested in Stinson's craft, a Sopwith biplane, especially its power plant, the Gnome rotary engine salvaged from the wreckage of Lincoln Beachey's fatal crash into San Francisco Bay. The motor had been recovered along with the body. Art recalled wit-nessing the dead spin into the bay during the Panama-Pacific Exposition. Beachey's monoplane disintegrated, flung hundreds of fractured pieces, flying components, gear, wings all around him. Now here was the very Gnome engine powering Stinson's Pup. What emotions must that somber tableau of the two grounded American fliers have inspired in the throng of curious Japanese citizens huddling there, the rain rattling the canvas roof of the hangar? They were the two survivors of the club, including Beachey, that had originated the loop-to-loop. Later, when the weather lifted, the show went on. The two agreed to perform together. Smith rigged a floor oil feed though Stinson's exhaust, allowing her to skywrite with him. They took off together, splashing through the rain-soaked field, startling the scattering herds of the heavenly sika deer of Nara as they gained speed. Their coordinated aerial acrobatic maneuvers mirrored the "dogfighting" taking place worlds away. On the ship passage to the East this time, Art Smith had been distracted by the back issues of the *New York World* newspaper in the ship's stateroom and the new puzzle it featured called "Word-Cross," where clues led the contestant to enter letters into blank squares of a diamond-shaped template. He was frustrated, however, discovering that most of the puzzles had been solved, the letters left in their spaces by the thoughtlessness of previous readers. Katherine Stinson was also familiar with the new puzzle craze and was eager to contribute to the simultaneous composition. The "O" hinge, created as the two circled each other elegantly over and over, confused the gaping crowd gazing up from below. Who was the pursued and who the pursuer?

Instructions in War Time

Upon hearing the news of the United States entering the Great War in April of 1917, Art Smith, The Bird Boy of Fort Wayne, immediately presented himself to the Aviation Section of the United States Signal Corps, the branch of the Army charged with organizing the country's first air force. His attempt to enlist as a combat pursuit pilot failed. He was thought to be unfit for flying, too short at five foot two to reach the pedals of the fighter craft and hobbled by the many injuries derived from his frequent crashes. He walked with a pronounced limp. His right arm at the shoulder demonstrated a limited range of motion. Several fingers of his right hand were numb. A big toe had been amputated after being frostbitten. His ears registered a constant ringing. The Aviation Section recognized the talent of the famous pilot nonetheless, and he was appointed a civilian instructor, reporting to Langley Field in Virginia. Instructor Art Smith quickly modified his Curtiss JN-4 training aircraft to accept his skywriting apparatus. Here, he used the device to simulate the sun in order to teach his new charges the tactic of using the sun's light to blind the enemy aviators under attack. The new pilots dove repeatedly out of this artificial sun. One was to be aware of where the sun was at all times, to employ it upon attacking, and to be conscious of its danger when on the defensive. Often, the simulation of THE SUN would become unreadable when backlit by the sun, the ethereal letters obliterated and overwhelmed with intense illumination from the higher altitude.

Art Smith, relegated to the pilot instructor role by a skeptical Army Air Force, was not one to contribute only the bare minimum in his new assignment. He, unasked, devoted his genius as a mechanical engineer and his many skills as a mechanic to the emerging obstacles of training aviators and adapting their aircraft to the rigors of aerial combat. For many long hours at McCook Field, he studied the captured specifications of Fokker's synchronization for the timed firing of Vickers machine gun rounds in intervals between the rotating propeller blades, discovering, at last, a method to add a second forward-firing weapon to the borrowed British Bristol F.2 fighter. Smith is also credited with the ingenious innovation of dual controls, allowing the student and pilot access to two sets of independent control surfaces. He often used his skywriting to instruct. Here the message exhorts his charges to consider the proper aiming at the enemy target sporadically maneuvering ahead of the attacker on "his tail." Smith would allow the novice to grip the dead stick as he flew the intricate pattern of composition—the attitudes and trims, the angles of attack, the banks and rolls, the dives and climbs—in order to create, in his young charges, the muscle memory of evasion, the attractive grip of gravity, the empty weightlessness waiting at the pinnacle of a loop after the coup de grâce.

Art Smith became an expert handling phosphorus during his nightly aerobatic displays at San Francisco's Panama Pacific Exposition in 1915. During the Great War, fleets of German Zeppelins attacked London, arriving over the city at night in what is thought to be the first strategic aerial bombing campaign of a major city. Initially, projectiles from artillery or aircraft had little effect on the massive dirigibles, as the pressure maintained in the gas envelopes was only slightly higher than the ambient air. Punctures had little effect. It was only when incendiary rounds were developed to ignite the flammable lifting gas within did the airships fall prey to the counterattacking airplanes. Here, in a brilliant phosphorous script, Art Smith illuminates the night with a target for his young charges to attack using munitions coated with these volatile jackets of fiery phosphorus.

Years later, while flying with the Air Mail Service in Ohio, Art Smith was one of the first on the scene at the crash of the *USS Shenandoah* over Noble County. He was able to spot the wreckage. The remnants of shiny silvered fabric of its envelope were strewn on the ground, reflecting the moon's intense light, radiating full and high overhead, the thunderstorm that had so recently torn the airship to pieces now breaking apart, the storm clouds accelerating away to the northeast, revealing a night sky punctuated by the distant and barely visible stars.

Iced Air

Into the 1920s, Art Smith, The Bird Boy of Fort Wayne, flew the mail overnight from Cleveland, Ohio, to Chicago, Illinois, in a de Havilland biplane he modified himself to ward off the freezing temperatures at altitude. He rigged the open cockpit with a canvas cowling that he cinched at his neck to deflect the blasting wind, and, at his feet, a shroud taken from an automotive exhaust heater radiated the soothing warmth given off by his 400 horsepower Liberty engine. He flew in relative comfort through the dark nights while during the day he moonlighted, composing advertising messages with his novel skywriting invention.

In the summer of 1922, in the midst of the record heat wave that would last through July, Art Smith climbed through the cloudless but dense tropic inversion over the Cuyahoga to etch in the saturated sky the promise made by the recently formed Carrier Engineering Corporation of mechanical "air conditioning."

Willis Carrier, the company's founder, was granted U.S. patent No. 808897 for his invention, which he named an *"Apparatus for Treating Air."* Carrier was by then the father of Rational Psychrometrics having first proposed the idea of a "relative" humidity, describing the difference between the actual temperature and the temperature one actually feels. Mr. Carrier had shown great interest in Smith's innovative skywriting and climate control devices, and they discussed, before the aviator's launch, the thermic degrees and gradations as one leaves the surface of the earth.

Over a steamy Cleveland, Art Smith dotting the "i" of the "i" in "iced" and the "i" of the "i" in "air" was freezing as he skated through thinning thermal layers. Below, he attempted to warm himself with memory, remembered it was sweltering there on the ground. His pristine calligraphy aloft no doubt was diffused by the oppressive haze hugging the earth. As he worked, his fingers going numb on the wheel and throttle, he imagined the solid column of stagnant air rising up to meet him from below, a thermal swirling, a kind of massive baking cake, and he a pastry chef, spelling out, in a frosty frosting and against his natural inclinations, a wished-for wish.

Influenza

It was once believed the sudden but cyclical reoccurrence of the respiratory disease we know as "the flu" was brought on by the periodic orbiting of heavenly bodies. The Italian word, "influenza" reflected this suspected connection that the radiation generated by the stars "influenced" the health and well-being of its earthbound recipients.

In the early months of 1918, a pandemic influenza swept the globe. It has become known as the "Spanish Flu," not because of its origin there but because Spain, a neutral country in the Great War, did not censor the morbidity and mortality rates as the disease took hold, creating the appearance that the flu persisted there and not within the borders of its combatant neighbors. In reality, one of the earliest outbreaks occurred in Haskell County, Kansas, in March of 1918.

Art Smith, The Bird Boy of Fort Wayne, then an instructor and test pilot for the United States Army Air Service, was dispatched from McCook Field in Dayton, Ohio, to Fort Riley, Kansas, where most of the camp was stricken by this novel and deadly strain of the disease.

In an attempt to quarantine the decimated post while at the same time disguising the true nature and extent of the calamity and its casualties, Smith inoculated the sky arching over Fort Riley with this homonymic message. In the still pristine air over the prairie, the message persisted, could be read for miles. Unbeknownst to the incapacitated bivouacked below, the chemical makeup of the smoke had been altered, infused with a tincture of antiseptic Listerine in aerosol suspension. Its heavier-than-air hygienic ingredients separated out of the solution of shaped sterile clouds over the time it took to construct the word, rained down silently and invisibly upon the congregation of the ill and their beleaguered caregivers barely surviving on the infected ground beneath Smith's feverish inscription.

At McCook Field, Art Smith had worked with engineer, Etienne Dormoy, on the early experiments in crop dusting, hauling aloft payloads of lead arsenate slurry to aerially apply the poison over a catalpa tree farm near Troy, Ohio. The target was a hawk moth, the catalpa sphinx caterpillar infesting the grove. The initial results seemed successful, the heavy metal mist being breathed in by the bugs' accordion-like spiracles, wreaking havoc on its respiratory function, and plating their colorful carapaces with a grimy metallic coating that knocked them from the defoliated branches.

Flying over Kansas, Art Smith watched as, in the great distance, clouds piled up into the spectacular anvil-headed vaporous mountain ranges of an approaching front, the silent lightning within it tripping a telegraphy of bright bursts throughout the long line of relentless weather. Indeed, the dead and dying below were "under the weather." And above it, in the thick occluded air, Art Smith, a devout Christian Scientist, circled and banked and dove and dipped, composing his kind of prophylactic prayer, an efficacious message to intercept and countermand the ill influences of that heaven domed above him. Seeded within the smoke, backlit by the green sunset filtered through the storm, sanded phosphorus ignited and oxidized, glittering as it burned within the words, creating a kind of smokescreen as the letters smeared into one another, propelled by the wind before the front. The writing became a silt of smoke, a fine flashing osmotic canopy of dust, another cloudy riddle absorbed into the approaching mass of clouds.

Still

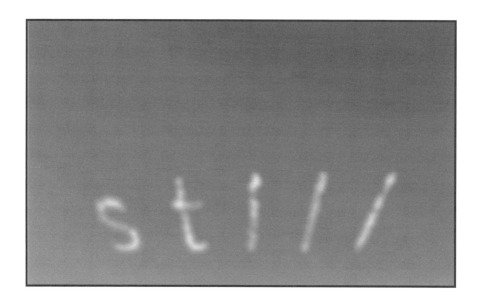

In 1915, on the eve of his departure from San Francisco to Japan for his first tour there, the news broke that Aimee Cour, the wife of Art Smith, The Bird Boy of Fort Wayne, had left California, returning home via train to her parents in Indiana. His three-year marriage in shambles, Art took to the air in pursuit of his retreating wife, tracing the railroad right-of-way until he overtook the consist near Truckee as her train approached the Donner Pass in the Sierra Nevada. There, in the thin mountain air, Smith composed a message in the hope his estranged wife would catch a glimpse of the missive out of her parlor car window.

Leap-frogging across the Great Central Plains, Art Smith followed the Overland Route of the Union Pacific, its crack express train bearing Aimee Cour eastward. Flying ahead of the speeding engine, Smith continued to skywrite this cryptic message at intervals that many on board, looking out from the open observation platform, believed mimicked, as it faded in the distance, the parade of telegraph poles, disappearing, as well, in the wake of the onward speeding train.

In Chicago, Aimee Cour changed trains, boarding the Pennsylvania Railroad's Broadway Limited to Fort Wayne. Art Smith flew between the city's tall buildings, etching in vapor the single word again, the same one he had inscribed over and over upon the open sky of two thirds of the North American Continent. His estranged wife must have spied the ghostly aerial letters sliced apart by the sculpted airspaces the skyscrapers created as her taxi, in lunchtime traffic, transferred her from the North Western Terminal to Union Station where she barely made her connection.

Years later, Art Smith, returned to Lake James in the northwestern corner of the state of Indiana. It was there, years before, drifting in a rowboat with his future wife, Aimee Cour, on the lake's placid surface that he confessed his love for her and his desire to fly, drawing her attention to the lazily circling hawk in the distance. As he hovered above the site, steering his smoke emitting aircraft to compose, once again, his plaintive message, Art Smith thought he remembered the moment that marked the beginning of his life. He once again spelled out the plea from years before. The letters overhead were reflected in the green waters of the lake and seemed to sink as they dissipated, disappearing below the jagged horizon of pine, the only sound that of his machine's echoing engine.

Mayday, Mayday, Mayday

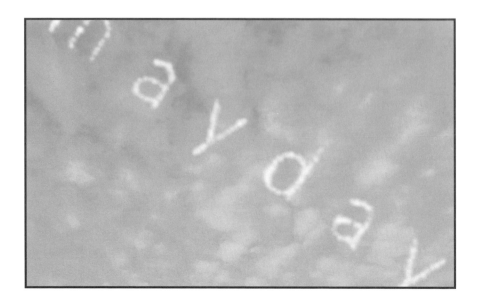

It is not known if this message that appeared over farm fields near Muncie, Indiana, in the spring of 1923, was actually meant to be a distress signal, but it is confirmed that Art Smith, The Bird Boy of Fort Wayne, was at the controls of the Curtiss JN-4 "Jenny" that applied it to the cloudless skies.

Earlier that year, Fredrick Mockford, the senior radio officer at London's Croydon Field, popularized the phrase, a corruption of the French *venez m'aider*, as a verbal equivalent of telegraphy's SOS. The proper procedure was to pronounce "mayday" three times in succession, MAYDAY, MAYDAY, MAYDAY, to distinguish it as an actual declaration of an emergency and not a message about a MAYDAY declaration. In any event, only one MAYDAY appeared that day in white smoke against the background of the azure skies of Indiana.

Art Smith had, by this time, crashed many times while piloting various aircraft, most famously his elopement flight and the botched landing at Osaka, and survived. At this point in his life, he was routinely flying mail between Cleveland and Chicago. It will be three more years before he mistakes the lights of a farmhouse for that landing field at night and plows into a copse of trees and perishes in the resulting fire.

That May Day, he flew in Troy, Michigan, during Fort Custer's Americanization Day parade, dropping confetti on the troops of the recently repatriated Russian Expeditionary Force as they passed in review. He performed his old aerobatic maneuvers for the appreciative crowd— endless loop-to-loops, traced by the curlicue of ragged smoke that might have looked as if he was in some kind of distress, stalled, on fire, and about to lose all control.

We lose track of Art Smith after that until he reappears again in our records, skimming over Indiana at treetop level. Below him, a ground fog of dust aroused by farmers breaking open the soil for spring planting. Beasts of all sorts scatter and stampede through the pastures beneath the Jenny, propelled by the engine's persistent trill. Perhaps the smell of the earth reaches the altitude, finds its way into the cockpit, freshening the thick stench of burnt engine oil and paraffin. It is a kind of accident that he is here now at the confluence of the seasons, of history, on his way home or off on some new adventure. The new leaves in the stretching trees just catching the sun are almost ready to explode.

$\mathcal{O}$

In the spring of 1916, Art Smith, The Bird Boy of Fort Wayne, embarked for Japan. Invited by the Emperor's government, he was to conduct a series of flights in that country, demonstrating the capabilities of the new flying machines. At the Panama Pacific Exposition, the year before, he had taken a Japanese flag with him on one of his many flights over the fair, commemorating, he announced, the ascension of the Mikado to the Imperial throne the next day. At 3,000 feet, in honor of the coronation taking place across the Pacific, he launched the banner. Attached to a "parachute," a new device of his own design, the flag unfurled, the banner floating to earth in an impressive diplomatic display. A year later, back in San Francisco, Art Smith circled above the Embarcadero, composing this farewell message as on the ground below his second biplane was loaded aboard the *Chiyomaru* along with a half dozen miniature racers he christened his "baby cars." In Japan, he would employ the speeders on the ground as part of his presentations. He completed several other aerial maneuvers that day, tracing with a trail of smoke as he emerged from the massive fog bank at the bay's entrance, an arch that, years later, would be realized with the span of the Golden Gate Bridge. Art Smith landed his plane on a nearby dock and proceeded to disassemble the craft, packing it carefully for safe storage aboard the steamer for the voyage.

O

During the lengthy voyage across the Pacific, Art Smith kept busy preparing for the exhibition that lay ahead. Several times, he tore down and rebuilt the mechanism that produced the smoke needed to generate skywriting, adjusting the apertures of the various nozzles, calibrating the coiled heating elements, and experimenting with new formulas of dyes and paraffin. In the early morning, the sun rising roundly in the ship's wake, he might be found on the fantail, launching any number of kites and gliders into the stiff prevailing headwind. The experimental craft, tethered to the ship's stern, performed startling aerobatics, guided by the sure touch of Smith's piloting, only to be reeled in later so as not to interfere with the late morning skeet shooting. Souvenir postcards were produced of Art Smith motoring one of his miniature race cars around the promenade deck of the *Chiyomaru*; copies would be sold later at the appearances in Japan. When not writing letters home, Smith busied himself sketching the schematics of his upcoming aerial compositions, reproduced here from the undated pages of his journal:

O

Sketched roughly on one page

o

and then revised on the following one.

0

And this image was found later in his notes.

~~~~

This scribble above was thought by many to be an innocent doodle, though it could represent an attempt to visualize some heretofore unrealized aeronautic maneuver.

Fellow passengers reported that they witnessed Smith transfixed at the ship's rail, observing through the circular frame of the ship's life-saving buoy the framed image of the apparently stationary but roiling mountains of ashy clouds emitted by the many active volcanoes of the Hawaiian Island chain hard by the ship's stately passage.

Upon landing at the Port of Yokohama, Art Smith oversaw the unloading of his crated biplanes. After the initial cursory customs inspections of the crates, the tarped and netted pallets of his cargo, Smith entertained a brief ceremonial welcome conducted by representatives of the prefecture's government, presenting The Bird Boy of Fort Wayne with feathered leis, laurel wreaths, and nosegays of local flowers while a local industry band played a far eastern rendition of "On the Banks of the Wabash Far Away." The welcoming crowd did not disperse but remained to watch the American aviator assemble one of his airships on the milling dock in the shadow of the *Chiyomaru*. Night fell as Smith worked to rebuild his craft, acquiring through such exertion his "land legs" once more. Upon completion of the task and after sufficient fuel was procured and delivered via a makeshift bucket brigade, Smith reviewed the working order of his engine in a static test there on the dock, the propeller revving loudly. And as the night came on, he decided to take a short shakedown sortie over the bay. In the gloaming overhead, Smith initiated his skywriting mechanism and in one continuous loop inscribed on the sky an O in a white smoke that appeared, to the amazed onlookers below, as black, backlit by the setting sun.

Art Smith, The Bird Boy of Fort Wayne, was given special permission to fly over the *Aoyama Itchome*. Tradition in Japan held that no mortal could be "higher" than the Emperor who with the Crown Prince and his brothers admired Smith's initial letter as it appeared overhead. That letter "O," to the surprise of Westerners in the party, was the only one forthcoming. In the pristine air it floated there, expanding slowly above the imperial grounds while Smith went on to perform various other loops and rolls no longer punctuated by a trail of smoke. At one point dropping perpendicularly 1,000 meters and pulling up at an altitude where he could easily be seen, he tipped his hat to the enthralled royal party a stone's throw below.

Immediately apparent to the enthusiastic and appreciative local audience, the circle of smoke was not a letter at all but a Japanese word, the *enso*, meaning circle itself and used in meditative calligraphy of *zen* to symbolize an "expression of a moment." One continuous brush-stroke, usually drawn with black ink on silk paper, was done here with the same elegance and grace in oily smoke upon the bleached blue sky over the Mikado.

The night sky in Kyoto was alive with fireflies. There above the sparks, Art Smith composed a new *enso*. This time he deployed the skywriting apparatus that used phosphorus to trace a blinding white circle in the inky sky. Later, it was reported in *Asahi shimbun* that Smith had said he performed the act while his eyes were closed. He had been blinded that night by the battery of searchlights on the ground following his every move.

This *enso* appeared over Osaka.

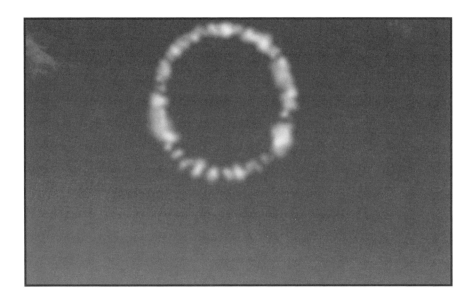

In Sapporo after inscribing an *enso* in a cloudless sky, Smith plummeted earthward in a "dead dive" from 400 meters, leveling overhead to race with the four midget cars jockeying below him when, suddenly, his engine seized. Gliding now, Smith attempted to steer clear of the crowd, avoiding injuring the startled spectators. His propeller stopped, Smith lost all control, and a gust of wind turned the biplane over into the ground. The fracture of his left leg would be a clean one. General Nagoake, his host, rushed to the disintegrated craft, scraps of the plane's canvas skin skidding along the new mown grass of the field caught up in the wind as it freshened.

Thin

The make of the altimeter used by Art Smith, The Bird Boy of Fort Wayne, was a Tycos. The inscription on its face read: SHORT & MASON, LTD. LONDON. Art Smith modified the instrument, soldering wire on the back of the case to create loops allowing for a leather strap to be threaded through the openings so that the device might be worn on his wrist. The altimeter measured altitude by means of gauging the atmospheric pressure, the vast mass of the air weighing down upon the earth. Art Smith referred to the air at the altitude where he did his work skywriting as "thin." Up there, he said many times, he felt a great weight lift off of him. He would float, he reported, as he nosed his airplane earthward whilst attaining the highest point on the arc of the terminal "n."

Often, Art Smith, The Bird Boy of Fort Wayne, would attempt to map the density of the various layers he would sense embedded in the wind stream. Flying through the clear clean air, he marked the gradients of the many transitions through the thinning atmosphere with the tell-tale epitaphs of smoke generated by his skywriting machine, mirroring the wispy strands of cirrus clouds floating even farther above the diminishing messages, a kind of airy moth-eaten parchment written upon by disappearing ink.

Art Smith would many times trace the seam between the high and low pressure systems he found aloft, a topography through the clouds, a vector demarcating the leading edge of the front's face often traveling for miles to the point that the fuel feeding his skywriting apparatus ran out. On one such occasion upon the exhaustion of that fuel, Art Smith noticed that the plane itself was producing a similar airy vapor from the vortices of wind his wings created. He dubbed the thin trails of smoke "contrails," a kind of elongated cloud generated by the moisture in the air, condensed when forced over the wing at high altitudes and high speed. He thought then of course of the aerial combat of the Great War, its Armistice recently concluded, and another kind of cursive line airplanes emitted—the oily smoke of burning fuel ignited by machine gun fire, the spiral punctuation mark written with gravity's grave hand, the emphatic gesture underlining this withdrawn miracle flight in the transparent medium of the sky.

At great heights and at such distances, the inviolable laws of perspective dictated the appearance of this skywriting over Fort Wayne in the summer of 1922. The hairbreadth needle pointer of Art Smith's altimeter swept over the instrument's inner dial. That face was scaled to a barometer, measuring pressure in pounds per square inch. The outer dial's scale, meshed with the bezel, was calibrated in feet and was rotated to score the elevation of the launching at the time and place of take off. Fort Wayne is 810 feet above sea level. Smith's altimeter, its crystal cracked and its case scorched from the fire of his final flight, was recovered along with the locket containing a strand of his mother's hair, slightly singed. The altimeter was found, upon its repair in 1950 by James Wigner, to be miscalibrated, off by nearly three hundred feet.

Birth

This movie still was taken from the silent film short documenting the release of the major motion picture *The Birth of a Nation* in 1915. Art Smith, The Bird Boy of Fort Wayne, was hired by Epoch Productions, the film's distributor, to advertise its release and grand opening in Los Angeles with this display of the new skywriting. D. W. Griffith, the director of *The Birth of a Nation* as well as its documentary short, is considered a pioneer of American cinema and an inventor and innovator of many film techniques including panoramic long shots, iris effects, night photography, color tinting, panning, and staged battle sequences where hundreds of extras are made to look like thousands. He was impressed upon hearing of Art Smith's creation of the aerial effect of skywriting and was anxious to use it in his film's promotion and to film the actual event of its application. The short documentary, now lost, is thought to be the first filmed evidence of skywriting as it is being written.

Nothing

In 1902, Dr. Charles Otis Whitman, a zoologist of Chicago University, in an attempt to reverse the catastrophic collapse of the wild passenger pigeon population, sent a captive breeding pair to the Cincinnati Zoo in the hope that a rock dove there would foster the distracted passenger pigeons' eggs. In 1910, Professor Whitman, working in his laboratory attempting to describe *Columbicola extinctus*, a louse thought at the time to be unique to the passenger pigeon and disappearing as the host species disappeared, caught a chill and died. Four years later, Martha, one of Dr. Whitman's birds, died in Cincinnati, becoming the endling of her species. Shortly before that, the zoo, in a vain hope, commissioned Art Smith to survey the Wabash and Maumee watersheds of Indiana, serving as a scout in what was to be the final wild passenger pigeon round-up. For several weeks, he scoured the river valleys in search of any evidence of a tattered covey of the pigeon that was thought to have numbered in the billions only half a century earlier. Then, Audubon lost count of the number of flocks, flocks made up of millions of individuals, when he attempted to record their passage near Louisville. "The air,"

he writes in *Birds of America*, "was literally filled with pigeons; the light of noon-day was obscured as by an eclipse; the dung fell in spots, not unlike melting flakes of snow; and the continued buzz of wings had a tendency to lull my senses to repose..." The skies over Indiana were now empty as Art Smith flew through them. As he banked his airplane, composing the O, he thought, perhaps, of the egg he had been shown, preserved in the collection of fossils and feathers at the funereal zoo. Years later, in 1947, long after Art Smith had died and was buried, the naturalist Aldo Leopold would compare the disappeared flocks to "a living wind." Art Smith began to climb, climbing by means of a spiral ascent, in long wide-open circles. Leveling off at last, he could see the horizon all around him. He was high enough to make out the initial warping off in the distance, the curvature of the earth, its promised declivity. As he lined up his craft again and began the application of smoke to cross the T, he experienced, suddenly, a patch of rough air, a turbulence, invisible, that, nevertheless, from its sheer force of downdraft, aberrated his plotted course, spoiling the capitalization, abrading the message he was attempting to send through all that empty emptiness.

Roses

1914. The Great War begins in Europe. There, it quickly becomes evident that the utter devastation meted out by modern weaponry will be so pervasive as to lay desolate the great rose gardens of Europe. 1915. That spring, hybridists of all the Major Powers meet secretly in Switzerland to discuss the creation of a grand refuge for the flower far from the lethal battlefields and the now newly aerially bombed cities. Meanwhile, half a world away in Philadelphia, Art Smith, The Bird Boy of Fort Wayne, is engaged by rose enthusiast, George C. Thomas, later Captain Thomas of the United States Army Air Service, to initiate a campaign of public awareness and fund raising for the creation of such a botanical refuge in one of the far western states. Art Smith takes to the air after adapting his skywriting mechanism to produce a deep red effluent, imploring the curious onlookers to cultivate the most beloved bloom.

Smith and Thomas also modified Smith's aeroplane to carry a cargo of rose petals, an apparatus mostly constructed of a netted hamper that when agitated proceeded to expel the petals. During a prolonged sweeping turn along the Schuylkill, Smith released his delicate cargo, creating, what was reported at the time, a crimson signature of flowers, a blood-red cloud curtain evocative of the noble carnage being spilled on the denuded plains of France and Belgium. The flowering trees along the river were in bloom, and the remnants of the raining rose petals clung to the native blossoms for days later until they too fell to the ground mixed with the now blown and spent native display.

Upon his return to the United States after his first successful tour of Japan in 1916, Art Smith, The Bird Boy of Fort Wayne, took to the air once more. His severe injury—a broken femur, sustained in the spectacular crack-up at Sapporo—was on the mend. He headed east, on several missions, one of which was to resuscitate the neglected drive to establish a sanctuary for rose propagation far from the botanical gardens of war-torn Europe.*

---

* In the spring of 1918, the rose cultivars began arriving in Portland, Oregon, soon to be known as the "City of Roses." The site of The International Rose Test Garden would grow to over four acres of terraced plots and sculptured beds. There would be nearly 10,000 plants and 600 varieties represented including the *Rosa kordesii* Rupert Brooke, named for the poet who died on his way to Gallipoli and is buried on the Greek island of Skyros. Art Smith, a long-standing proponent of the rose refuge, was transporting a bare root Rupert Brooke start with him as he installed the evocative message, above, in the dirty weather over Portland.

Again, he flew to Philadelphia to assist George Thomas in his campaign. This time he composed a message that extended the length of the Delaware River waterway, the airy letters drifting as they dissipated in the prevailing breeze decaying over the far reaches of the New Jersey shore. Once more, Smith followed, in the wake of the desiccating inscription, with an infusion of iridescent petals that drew a shimmering curtain in front of the setting sun. The petals were so buoyant and the drafts of air that day so stirring that the shower Smith unleashed seemed to levitate instead of falling. Stalling, it continued to rain down through the gloaming, giving Smith enough time to land his aeroplane on the Jersey waterfront and enjoy the sparkling drizzle of fragrant confetti. Unbeknownst to Art Smith that day, his craft served as an unwitting vector for an insidious invader. Concealed within the precipitation of roses was a stealthy stowaway transported from Japan, its eponymous beetle, *Popillia japonica*, that copper-colored clumsy flier discovered and scientifically confirmed a few months after Art Smith's departure by a Rutgers entomologist in a Riverton, New Jersey, florist's greenhouse.

The Moon

With the commencement of the Volstead Act in 1920, Art Smith, The Bird Boy of Fort Wayne, found himself between ruminative situations. Recently demobilized from the U.S. Army Air Service and yet to be hired by the Post Office to inaugurate the fledgling Air Mail Service in the Midwest, Smith offered his skills to the beleaguered Treasury Department's Bureau of Prohibition in the eradication of alcoholic spirits being smuggled across the Great Lakes from Canada. Operating from the stable platform of a surplus Royal Aircraft Factory F.E.2 fighter-bomber, he circled above the Maumee River as it meandered through the verdant valley from Fort Wayne to the port of Toledo on Lake Erie. Having modified his craft to deploy the phosphorescent night skywriting script, he illumined the coastal marshes, confluences, and estuaries affording egress to the lighters launched from the ships offshore or the commandeered car floats of the Canadian National Railroad.

Lucky

Documentation of this skywriting may be found in a letter from Art Smith, dated October 28, 1923, to Garnet Straits of Flat Rock, Michigan. He asks if she or any friends or family saw the message floating over Detroit that summer. Art had met Garnet by chance a year before when his de Havilland mail plane had to set down, making a forced landing in the Straits family pasture. Art stayed with the Straits during the time it took to make repairs on the aircraft, striking up an acquaintance with the eighteen-year-old Garnet that soon bloomed, in the days that followed, into mutual admiration and affection. The relationship matured and blossomed. It is said that the couple was even engaged to be wed but for the fatal crash of 1926. Buoyed by the frequent exchange of letters that Art Smith would sometimes "deliver," launching a bundle of missives over the house in Flat Rock once he deviated from his route between Cleveland and Chicago, Garnet was to say years later of Art Smith, The Bird Boy of Fort Wayne, that it seemed as if "he dropped out of heaven."

The Falling Leaf

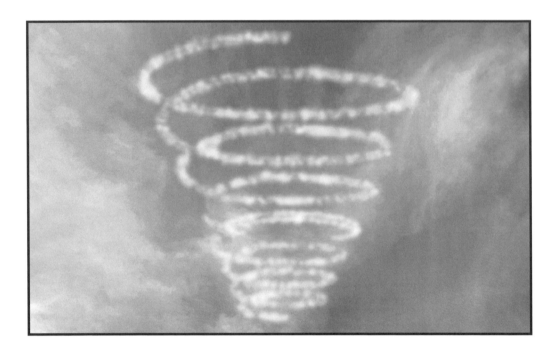

He called it "The Falling Leaf," Art Smith, The Bird Boy of Fort Wayne, did. He had, many times, descended from altitude by such means, employed a spiral trajectory, either narrowing the loops as he approached the earth or widening the loops as he fell. In all those initial attempts in early aerobatics, however, he was unable to record the graceful decline; map the difficult maneuver in order for an audience to appreciate these daring initial experiments in the physics of controlled powered flight. In other words, the onlookers were unable to tell "the dancer from the dance" to quote W. B. Yeats, a poet Art Smith was known to admire. Perhaps this lack of the ability to inscribe the complicated exertion against and in tandem with gravity, circling through the transparent air, incited Smith to create "skywriting" in the first place! "The Falling Leaf" is seen here in the December night sky of 1915 at San Francisco's Panama-Pacific Exposition. To record the stunt that night, he used intense light tracings that would score the overexposed photographic negatives of the under-illuminated event. He accomplished it by using burning phospho-rescent fusees borrowed from the Southern Pacific Railroad Company, an extremely dangerous combustible to have on board his wood and canvas aircraft. The leaf he was thinking of, I think now, must have been the palm-sized maple leaf prevalent in his hometown in Indiana. And what with its fiery colors of autumn—the reds and oranges and yellows—a camouflage of flame while falling, the leaf, no doubt, suggested to him the pyrotechnical display he would create. I can see him now, trans-fixed, watching the whirling leaves landing one after one. Or, perhaps more accurately, he sought to mimic the motion of the cantilevered con-struction of the maple tree's winged seeds, double samaras, with their elegant helical transcriptions as they spun to the earth through the late summer's humid air. In any case, this stunt became Art Smith's signature, literally, written each night in the sky over the exposition.

It is the "graveyard spiral" but also known as the "vicious spiral," the "deadly spiral," or, simply, the "death spiral." This fatal spiral dive, ini-tiated, accidentally, when a pilot flying in fog, night, or other visually obscured phenomenon is blind to the horizon. The sensory deprived pilot listens to the signals, illusionary signals it turns out, emanating from the inner ear. He feels that he is in level flight but losing altitude and reacts (he cannot help himself) to pull up. But in doing so, he only tightens the turn, accelerating into the banking turn his plane is already locked into. It creates a kind of vertigo for the plane. But that vertigo is kept from the pilot in the blind cockpit where the instinctual maneuver of "pulling up" feels like life-saving equilibrium. Trusting one's "seat of the pants"

over the feedback of flight instruments, a pilot over-corrects. He gets the "leans," sensing he is level when he is not, he continues to compensate to the false whisper in his ear. It is paradoxical that the confused and confusing organ complicit in the service of the "death spiral" should be the inner ear with its corkscrewing cochlea and its braid of semicircular canals that sculpt in bone and tissue the very deadly flight path the ear fails to read or comprehend. Art Smith, The Bird Boy of Fort Wayne, trained with early, view-limiting devices, trained and then trained others to fly with instruments, to override the messages his own sensing apparatus mistakenly produced. Shown here, a controlled death spiral, very much like "The Falling Leaf" of San Francisco, over Dayton, Ohio, sometime after he began flying for the Mail Service. His "skywriting" transcribing, in a controlled manner, the nightmarish spiral for student observers on the ground. His own fatal crash, a few months later, would be ruled a pilot error. But it was a different kind of mistake, one of visual acuity not auditory derangement as he mistook the lights of a farmyard as aids to navigation at a landing field. Still, after all this time, a failure to recognize or respond to instrument readings is the most common cause of what we now call "a controlled flight into terrain."

It might have been that Art Smith, The Bird Boy of Fort Wayne, first read W. B. Yeats's poem "The Second Coming" in the magazine *The Dial* where it was first published in 1920. The Christian Science Reading Room in Fort Wayne did carry the magazine in its inventory out of the mistaken belief that it was still the Transcendentalist journal it was at its founding in 1840. Or did the book in which the poem was later collected, *Michael Robartes and the Dancer*, fall into his hands a year later in a Cleveland bookseller's shop or the Allen County Public Library between sorties for the Mail Service or applications of skywritten advertisements? He would have been taken by the imagery of flight and flying encapsulated by the falcon and falconer as well as the evocation of the "widening gyre" the bird turns through in the poem's opening line. The sublime apocalyptic symbolism would have struck a chord as the poem addresses the aftermath of The Great War's traumatic disruptions. The bombing of cities from the air. Aerial dogfighting with rapid firing machine guns diabolically designed to fire in the clear intervals between spinning propeller blades. Fiery midair disintegrations of fragile and unstably tuned aircraft. Smith and many veterans read the bleak verses generated by the carnage. Sassoon, Owen, Brooke, Graves. The early optimistic elation that airplanes and flying promised seemed broken and exhausted as aviation and Art Smith settled into routines of hauling bags of letters through the air punctuated by the prosaic tattooing of the sky with advertisements for cigarettes and shaving cream. The center not holding. This lyrical curlicue was captured over rural Zulu, Indiana, in the summer of 1922 amidst the circling turkey buzzards and quarreling crows. A folly of exhaustion? A distracted doodle? An attempt to recapture some of the spent joy of his boyhood flight? A transcription of a sigh? A hieroglyph of a death wish?

On Wednesday, March 18ᵗʰ, 1925, the deadliest tornado in the history of the United States cut through Missouri, Illinois, and Indiana. The Tri-State Tornado killed close to 700 and injured more than 2,000, damaging 20 cities, four of which were effaced from the earth. It was a fast moving storm, averaging 60 miles per hour as it moved diagonally from southwest to northeast. It traveled over 300 miles, in the five hours it was on the ground, carving a path that ranged from 1 to 3 miles in width. Had there been satellites, the ruled straight-edged course of the storm's destruction would have been visible from space. And even a few months after the event, that scored course remained visible to Art Smith, The Bird Boy of Fort Wayne, who, from a mere mile aloft, easily tracked the storm's irresistible vector as it plowed through the mostly rural landscape. The shadow of his Jenny fell on the actual trued black furrow in the fields below still papered with debris, tangled metal wreckage, alluvial fans of masonry, clapboard sticks, and swaths of shingles. At the end of his reconnoitering near Princeton, Indiana, where half the town was destroyed and the Heinz factory flattened, Smith pulled up, performed a slow circling climb into thinner and ever thinner air, probably not even aware that he had initiated the telltale smoke of his skywriting, and disappeared there, above a high ceiling of reddish cirrocumulus clouds also known as a mackerel sky.

Gas City

Serious mining of the natural gas reservoir, a reserve that would become known as the Trenton Field in east central Indiana, began in the late 1880s. Overnight, thousands of wells were drilled. The deposits of fossil fuel in the huge interconnected field spread over 5,000 square miles, nearly the size of the state of Connecticut, and contained a trillion cubic feet of gas and a billion barrels of oil. To prove that the gas was flowing from the new well bores, the operators tapped the mainline, piping off a portion of the flow to set the surplus spectacularly ablaze. The flames towered over the plains and prairies, forests of fire. The flares could be seen as far north as Fort Wayne. And the light over the horizon above Indianapolis roiled and flickered, a man-made display of the aurora borealis. These constantly combusting gas flares came to be known as "flambeaux." The discovery led to an industrial boom for commerce, illumination, manufacturing, especially of glass products. Ball Brothers, Henry, Hoosier, Root, and Sneath—all these companies were attracted by the cheap and seemingly inexhaustible fuel. Art Smith, The Bird Boy of Fort Wayne, began his flying career just as the great gas field of Indiana was reaching its peak. Aloft, even in daylight, he could see over the horizon, south to the far reaches of Delaware, Jay, Blackford, and Grant Counties and the copses of yellow orange flames flaring in the distance, the light seemingly floating, like oil on the shimmering melting azure of liquefied air. At night, the flambeau-burning created a deep blue mirage, a blanket that wavered like waves on a black sand shore. In 1912, the Chamber of Commerce of Gas City hired Smith to celebrate The Boom by writing BOOM over the booming city ringed with flaming groves and arbors of flambeaux whose jets of combusting gases leapt up toward Smith's vapory writerly combustion, fingers pointing, twitching flickering hands grasping the slowly expanding, ever thinning rings of the mute BOOM.

Only a few years later, Art Smith, The Bird Boy of Fort Wayne, returned to the famous Trenton Gas Field on a more sober mission of sky calligraphy. The pressure across the field was falling. The decline in pressure meant that the gas to heat the houses and power the furnaces of Indiana would soon be too low to continue flowing. At the turn of the century the pressure at the wellheads was near 200 psi. By the time of Smith's initial visit, the flow had fallen to 150 psi and continued to fall. It was suspected, even then, that the open displays of flame were a major contribution to the rapid depletion of what was thought to be a vast and bottomless resource. Now, a century later, we understand that as much as 90% of the field's natural gas was wasted in flambeau displays. And much of the proved oil reserve, without the pressurized gas to aid in its extraction, remains below the Hoosier bog unlifted and unliftable. In 1916, Smith was invited back to Indiana (from his triumphant turn at the Panama-Pacific Exposition in San Francisco where he had lit up the night with skywriting, produced by means of phosphoric flares) to commemorate the extinguishing of the final flambeau. The fire forests of standing pipe, burning continuously for a quarter of a century, now saw their arboreal canopy of flame dwindling, going out, extinguished. The Chamber of Commerce at Gas City did not want to wait for what now seemed inevitable, but instead sought to ceremonially cap what was believed to be the last flambeau. This they did as Art Smith arched over the funereal crowd below. He considered writing, "DOUSE" or "DONE" or "ENOUGH' or "SNUFF" or "OVER." He wanted to find a word that would suggest the blowing out of candles on a birthday cake, onomatopoeia of exhaustion, exhalation, breath, a whooshing whispered wish. But he settled on a return to the optimistic BOOM of a few years before, transmuted to this startled interjection of the unexpected, the uncontrolled. The sun was setting as he took to the air. The Indiana State Seal depicts a sun near a mountainous horizon, a man with an ax felling a tree that a bison leaps over in flight. There was never much thought about the kind of sun that's pictured, setting or rising. But now? And the mountains in the distance, they never made sense, he thought, as he closed the last radii of his second zero and the faint sun sank through it toward the flat, hairline fracture that would be there in the diminished distance: Illinois.

Rest

The first publicly sponsored Fourth of July fireworks display in Fort Wayne took place at the Irene Byron Tuberculosis Sanatorium north of the city in the summer of 1925. The Sanatorium, opened in 1919, housed varying ages of infected patients in the then state-of-the-art facility. There were several buildings on the campus with one unit entirely dedicated to children. The fireworks were launched in such a manner that they could be viewed from the numerous screened-in verandas and sun porches where the patients daily enjoyed part of the generally accepted regimen of treatment—rest and more rest, steeping in rest, sleeping in fresh air both days and nights all year round. The patients also received a healthy diet and could partake in light exercise at the hospital's wading pool, playground, badminton courts, and table tennis tables. All were gathered on the porches, patios, and balconies that midsummer late gloaming, anticipating the pyrotechnics later that evening but now entertained by Art Smith, The Bird Boy of Fort Wayne, whose smoky prescription of R E S T was transformed as they watched into F R E S H,

[161]

the H appearing as a kind of pentimento, a hashed out H from the initial T. The image appeared all feathery, like the tail of the badminton cock. To the doctors present, the cylindrical shaped dashes and slashes of the manufactured clouds eerily reminded them of their microscopic viewing of the cultured bacillus, *M. tuberculosis*, glimpsed in its limpid laziness, stained red in the sputum on the pathological slides. The setting sun lit up the skywriting, embossing the letters to create an illusion of depth. The exhibit was greeted by a smattering of applause and the routine static of expectorate coughing from the excited residential patients.

Only months before, Art Smith, The Bird Boy of Fort Wayne, had been contracted by the Parker Brothers game company to advertise their acquisition in 1925 of the license and the right to use the name "Ping-Pong," the trademark of the J. Jaques & Sons Ltd company of Great Britain, for their line of table tennis equipment. Earlier that Fourth of July day, Smith replicated what might have been the first ever Legal Notice posted via skywriting when he discovered the many table tennis tables available to the patients of the Irene Byron Sanatorium. What he did not know was the celluloid Ping-Pong balls, whether Parker Brothers brand or not (I do not know), were also used therapeutically in the treatment of tuberculosis itself at the hospital. The pneumothorax technique allowed for the collapsing of the infected lung, allowing the infected tissue to "rest" by means of plombage. The collapse of the lung was created by inserting a bag filled with Ping-Pong balls into a cavity created beneath the upper ribs. I am unable to ascertain if the balls themselves were the same ones used in the matches ambulatory patients played on the grounds.

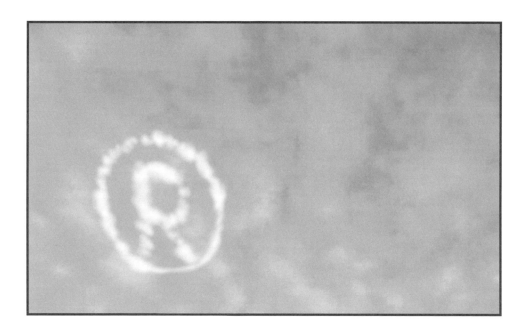

Although not officially recognized as the legal symbol for registered trademark until the Trademark Act of 1946, the ® was in informal use long before that. Smith enjoyed creating it while skywriting. Sometimes he would make the circle first and then ricochet around inside the boundary creating the capital R. Other times, he would reverse the maneuver, sketching out the letter and then enclosing it, trying to come as close as he could to the floating ligatures of thinning smoke. The ideograph, now that I think of it, might have represented the plombage, the cavity packed with an autonomic and organic sack of balls. Or was it the ball itself, a kind of plastic alveolus, its thin branded skin enveloping a vacuum. It didn't matter. He enjoyed the challenge of it, loved creating it, even considered registering the ® as a registered trademark of his own so that as he finished one giant mark in the sky he would conclude with a smaller one orbiting the first like a moon. And that made him think of the © and there, backlit by the first Fourth of July fireworks display of Fort Wayne, Indiana, dodging the flak clouds in the after-dark of the explosions of glittering light going on all around him, Art Smith, Fort Wayne's native son, copy-wrote this waxing crescent moon hanging over the suburban Fort Wayne near the village known as Huntertown.

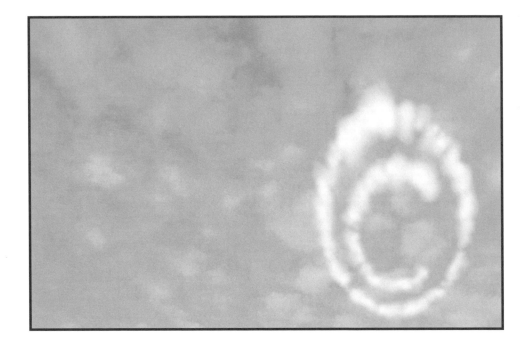

The Border

In 1913, Gideon Sundback, working as head designer for the Fastener Manufacturing and Machine Company in Meadville, Pennsylvania, invented the modern zipper. The name "zipper," however, was trade-marked by B. F. Goodrich Company, which coined the term when it added the fastener to its rubber galoshes in 1923. Seven years before that, Art Smith, The Bird Boy of Fort Wayne, stitched this advertising message onto the clear blue skies over Fort Bliss in El Paso, Texas. In 1916, the Fastener Manufacturing and Machine Company, having changed its name to Talon, was now aggressively marketing the device, and commissioned our skywriter to cryptically affix this tattoo over larger cities—especially those with military installations, armories, and quartermaster depots. Talon's thinking was (what with war raging in Europe and with the America's intervention there seeming inevitable) the expeditionary forces would need new modern efficient closures for their kits and caboodle. Art Smith designed the display himself having been mesmerized by the new, yet unnamed "zipper" now installed over his heart on a slash pocket of his double-breasted leather flying jacket for safe storing of his folded oilcloth maps. He pulled at the pull tab, running the slider up and down, admiring the sound of the contraption—its controlled tear, it rasp and ratchet—knitting and unknotting, a miracle, each tooth fitting into its diastema, a suture, laced fingers. He worried the design like a prayer and sewed up the sky in smoke.

Art Smith, The Bird Boy of Fort Wayne, was also known as The Crash Kid. There had been many crashes leading up to this afternoon spent knotting up the sky over El Paso. Not that he felt in any way in any peril that day. The aeronautics were relatively benign—the lazy figure 8 with the smoke extinguished through the radii of the wide banking turns. And his airplane that day, the reliable Curtiss JN-3, was an infinitely more stable platform than his homebuilt spit and baling wire Pushers. They had, more often than not, stuttered and stalled and slammed into the corn-stubbled ground or a canopy of unforgiving trees, a litany of being let down. He'd regain consciousness after a crash, the smoldering bamboo and balsa just beginning to catch and burn, and see his personal catastrophes—the gashes, the slick lacerations, the protruding tibia or fibula, looking to him, in shock, like the control sticks of his splintered aircraft. Ha! It would be something if the skin came equipped with such cunning little fasteners, slide the slice right up. A part of him wanted desperately to fly in the impending war, take off into the leading edge of experimental flight. Dogfights! Immelmanns! Tailslides! Hammerheads! But the fix was already in. The shattering and resettings of his legs and arms, his back, his fingers, his toes in all those crashes would wash him out of the Air Service when the time came. His feet would be unable to reach the pedals on the "Tommy" trainer. His arthritic hands would be unable to grasp the throttle on the Avro. But, in 1916, another war was knocking on the door—the Mexican Revolution across the border. In his landing approaches, he would swing out and around effortlessly through that alien airspace, banking over Juarez as the Revolution was entering its final phases below. And here he was on the border advertising new fangled notions for notions in an unraveling world.

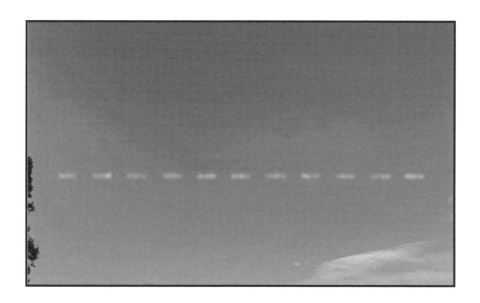

It hadn't been that long, a little over a year, that his companion in the celebrated aerial elopement and marriage, the love of his life, Aimee Cour, had left him in California and returned to the Midwest. Now, here on this extreme border, still smarting from that crash, he sought solace on the outer edges of what had been his known world. This was Art Smith's, The Bird Boy of Fort Wayne's, migration to mitigate those nagging injuries. He thought of his assignment here as a kind of banishment, forty days of wandering alone in the wilderness, the desert—the deserted desert itself and the wide deserted sky that seemed even wider than usual, endlessly cloudless, ever expanding, empty even of empty. After his daily skywriting, introducing to the quartermasters of Fort Bliss below the modern mechanism of closure, Art Smith would set a course along the international boundary, expending the last of his calligraphic fuel, tracing the sovereign demarcation, making visible, in his mind, an "us" and a "them," hoping to purse up all those feelings that constantly percolated within him. Oh, but even as he drew the drawstrings closed, irrational geography, he knew. He wasn't fooling himself.

He knew he was not of one place or the other but constantly between, in between the between. Heaven and Hell. America and Mexico. Day and Night. Flying and Falling. He left in his wake, always, a stuttering and impermanent imaginary geometry, a porous border made up of tenuous threads of fleeting gossamer, the gauziest of insubstantial clouds.

Eighty miles due west from El Paso, Art Smith, The Bird Boy of Fort Wayne, flew along the border to Columbus, New Mexico. It was March 19th. Ten days before, Pancho Villa and the remnants of his failing Army of the North had crossed the border, raiding Columbus, burning the train station and other buildings, killing seventeen Americans. Now, Columbus would become the rallying point for the Army's 1st Aero Squadron, eight JN-2s and eleven pilots, as they kicked off the Punitive Expedition in support of General Pershing's force of 6,600 already deep into Mexico searching for Villa. The planes, unarmed and underpowered for the high desert, were ordered to rendezvous with the ground forces in Casas Grandes 90 miles south into Mexico. Art Smith in his skywriting Jenny, circled, watching as the Army's airplanes lumbered into the air, too late in the day, into the gathering dusty darkness. They would be gone a year, looking for Villa and his raiders. Smith by then would be long gone, back up north, would hear of the spectacular failures of the aeroplanes and airmen—the wooden propellers delaminating in the dry heat, the crash landings in shifting sand, the radiator explosions spewing blood red water into the open cockpits. In Chihuahua City, Lt. Drague would be fired upon by four Mexican policemen with Winchester rifles, the first recorded attack on a U.S. military plane. But all of this would be forgotten. All of it eclipsed. The War in Europe would intervene in this intervention, calling Pershing and his troops over there instead. The Mexican Revolution would end in amnesty for Villa and his men. Villa himself would be assassinated years later driving home in his Dodge touring car to the hacienda in Canutillo by a pumpkinseed seller shouting *"Viva Villa!"* But all of that was from a different country, the undiscovered country of the Future. The next morning in Columbus, New Mexico, after the 1st Aero Squadron had disappeared into old Mexico, Art Smith headed back along the invisible border to El Paso, landing at Fort Bliss to share the news of the Expedition's incursion. Along the way he closed the door behind him, so to speak, posting something like a fence wire warning along the way, a patriotic gesture, he believed then, adorned with a few menacing X's, barbing the line in the sky. They were, he hoped, of such scale, such majesty, he imagined, no one would ever want to cross this way again, now or in that unknown future.

ABC

By 1922, in Indianapolis, the letters A B C no longer stood for "American Brewing Company" but now brought to the minds of the Circle City's citizenry the appellation of the town's famous Negro National League baseball team, originally sponsored by the brewery at its founding in 1913, now its own eponymous eponym. Art Smith, The Bird Boy of Fort Wayne, applied the alphabetic advertisement that summer's season circling above the Washington Baseball Grounds, just west of the White River, the field they shared with the Indianapolis Indians of the American Association. As he composed the gigantic quilt of letters, stitching each white abraded thread to the blue field of the sky, he sang the children's alphabet song—A B C D E F G...—partially to pass the time but also to keep time, the duration of the verse and its rests a kind of rally point, a sing-song metronome of time-keeping until the next turn or bank. He knew too that the melody was also the one used in "Twinkle, Twinkle, Little Star," and above him he could see, beyond the thinning veil of the atmosphere, mostly made pale in the bright sunlight, the quavering stars and twitching planets, maybe even the ethereal ghost of a gibbous washed-out membrane of the moon. The song too was the line on which was hung the lyric of "Baa, Baa, Black Sheep" and, as he left wondering about the location of the little star, he turned effortlessly to the number of bags of black wool the black sheep had for the master, the dame, and, descending, the little boy in the lane. Flying low now over the dusty diamond below he caught the teams hustling between innings, his plane seeming to herd the flock of wool-flanneled baseball players off the field, annotated with lullabies and nursery rhymes. Olivia Taylor, C. I. Taylor's widow, was now the owner of the ABCs, and the season would be a turnaround year. In the bleachers on the third-base side, she shielded her eyes with her gloved hand and inspected the elemental instructions and monumental inscription she had commissioned in the sky overhead.

It was Henry Chadwick, The Father of Baseball, who, once he had devised the box score for the game, suggested the letter "K" to designate a strikeout, arguing that "K" was the "most prominent" of the letters in the word "struck" and had a harmonic relationship with the boxing abbreviation "K.O." for "knockout." The "K" stuck. It continues to be used today as an indication of an out made by striking out. Purists will still reverse the letter to indicate that the strikeout was a result of a called strike instead of a swing and miss. This "K" captured over the Washington Baseball Grounds during another Indianapolis ABCs' game that year was a kind of swing and a miss. Mrs. Taylor had been so pleased with the earlier skywriting that she had commissioned Art Smith, The Bird Boy of Fort Wayne, to keep score in the sky. But this experiment seems to have been a disaster what with the measured pace of the game, the rudimentary communication from the field below, and the shifting wind all making for an illegible hodgepodge of drifting symbols, cyphers, and figures. And, finally, it did not seem to illuminate, in any significant way, or increase meaningfully the enjoyment of the game or the appreciation of the ABCs' play on the field that day against the Chicago American Giants.

One might imagine that the skywriting pictured above from the summer of 1922 was part of the failed sky scoring aloft during the Indianapolis ABCs' home game at the Washington Baseball Grounds. Of course, the official annotation for a walk is a "W" or the preferred "BB," standing for "Base on Balls," so it was curious that the more cumbersome W A L K would have been spelled during the disastrous attempt to record the competition below. Additional research has revealed that this W A L K, while applied above the bleachers during an ABCs game, was photographed in this incomplete state and captures only a partial rendering on its way to becoming a complete advertisement for the near west side enterprise of Madam C. J. Walker. The E and the R are yet to be generated. The C. J. Walker Company factory, at 640 North West Street, was a nearby neighbor. The company was the leading manufacturer of hair care products and cosmetic creams, shampoos, pomades, and irons. There also, it trained Madam Walker's "beauty culturists" in "The Walker System." Madam Walker herself had died in New York City three years before, the year of The Red Summer, 1919, but her legacy continued in

Indianapolis, the company run by her daughter, A'Lelia, who also would continue her mother's philanthropy, political activism and patronage of the arts in New York during the Harlem Renaissance. When A'Lelia died in 1931, she was buried next to her mother in Woodlawn Cemetery in the Bronx. At the interment, Hubert Julian, The Black Eagle, circled above in his modified Curtiss Jenny, dropping red gladiolas and dahlias on the mourners below. But years before that, in 1922, the very same summer Art Smith was writing in the skies over Indianapolis, Hubert Julian, The Black Eagle, was making his first flight over Harlem during the Universal Negro Improvement Association Convention, affixing to the sky various UNIA slogans. That year too, The Black Eagle had patented his "airplane safety appliance," a parachute combined with a rudimentary propeller. It is not known, and highly unlikely, if Art Smith was equipped that day with such a device. We can now, from the distance of this future time, see that this W A L K affixed over the ABC game in 1922 was also a kind of historic annotation as the Great Migration of African-Americans from the southern United States to the north was reaching its zenith. At the same time, the rural American population, of all colors, was moving into America's expanding cities. People were on the move and beginning to close distances and distort, though the inventions of speedy transport—cars, trains, and now, airplanes—time itself. Perhaps here is where the myth of baseball as a pastoral pastime set in the frenetic urban space began. Not the machine in the garden so much as the garden inside the furious infernal machine. In any case, Art Smith, The Bird Boy of Fort Wayne, circled, applying a kind of cosmetic adornment to the ordinary sky about the application of cosmetic adornment for the crowds below watching boys play a game in summer. It is said that beauty is only skin deep and that a picture is worth a thousand words, or in this case, a picture of one word seems to have been worth about a thousand more.

Allow me to return for a moment to that brooding K floating over Indianapolis in the summer of 1922 referred to above. As the reader knows or can, at least, intuit, Franz Kafka, a contemporary of Art Smith, The Bird Boy of Fort Wayne, was writing in Prague at this time, though not in the sky there. That year Kafka began work on a novel that would later, after his death in 1924, be published as *Das Schloss* (*The Castle*) whose featured character, named K. Kafka, too, was swept up in the zeitgeist of that era. It should come as no surprise that Kafka, in 1909, was in attendance at the famous Air Show at Brescia, Italy, publishing, that same year, the story fragment *"Die Aeroplane in Brescia"* in the newspaper *Bohemia*. It is said to be the first description of powered flight in the German language and its literature. In 1913, Kafka traveled with friends to Vienna, and there sat for the only photograph extant that pictures this important writer smiling.

I have searched through Kafka's published work to see if there is a reference to baseball. There is none that I could ascertain though in the incomplete finale of fantastic fragments in *Amerika* and its "Nature Theatre of Oklahoma," I did find something. There, the protagonist, Karl, in the almost limitless vastness of the valleys and hills, a pastoral paradise, adopts, strangely, the new name, "Negro."

On March 9th, 1915, at Daytona Beach, Florida, the famous pioneer aviatrix Ruth Law was to drop a baseball from 500 feet into the waiting catcher's mitt of future Hall of Famer, Wilbert Robinson. The story goes that Law left without the baseball and instead launched a grapefruit earthward, which then burst apart as it hit Robinson's glove. The red pulp, the stinging acid of the citrus fruit, led the catcher to believe that the baseball he thought was heading his way had injured him badly, blinding and bloodying him. Six years later, Art Smith, acquainted with his fellow flier, Ruth Law, who was the first to do the loop-to-loop, proposed to the ABCs' front office a similar stunt that summer. He would launch from above while circling over the Washington Baseball Grounds not one, not two, but three baseballs that would plummet into the waiting grasp of the team's outfielders below. By 1922, the art of aerial bombardment had been advanced immeasurably by the crucible of The Great War. Art Smith jettisoned the baseballs from an altitude of 500 feet, and they descended through the baffle of capital K's he had previously etched on the otherwise cloudless daylight skies over Indianapolis.

The balls accelerated, propelled by the constant attraction of gravity at thirty-two feet per second per second. Though there is an inevitability to this descent—one can imagine the spheroids approaching from the point-of-view of waiting targets growing larger and larger, backlit and looming as they drew closer—and the irresistibility time provides, the historic photographic record here creates the illusion of levitation and the paradox of an infinite regression. There! Did you catch it? Those motes, the minuscule specks of black suspended in midair? Are those the captured shadows of the plummeting balls? No, perhaps only a period-sized dot of dust that intervened between the negative and the fixing agent, a bubble in the emulsion. In any case, nothing else remains as evidence of that event. It was after all a stunt performed during a Negro Leagues doubleheader in a minor league town, during a time when acrobatic and barnstorming flight with all its wonders was just reaching its height, only a few summers from the stall, initiating its own parabolic descent, and the novelty turning toward endurance records and the competitions for altitude, speed, and the rewriting of history.*

---

* It should be noted that, simultaneously to the events recorded above, the Ku Klux Klan in Indiana, led by the notorious D. C. Stephenson was reaching its ascendancy that summer. The Indiana General Assembly passed legislation to create Klan Day at the Indiana State Fair, which included a nighttime cross burning. And on July 4th of the next year, there would be a rally of more than 100,000 in Kokomo.

Metro Day

July 15th, 1915, was Metro Day at the Panama-Pacific International Exposition in San Francisco, honoring the contributions the Metro Pictures Corporation had made to the fair. Francis X. Bushman, president of the company, led the Metro delegation through the throngs on the Avenue of Palms to the Court of the Universe where officials of the Exposition received them. Speeches were given and tokens exchanged. Edward A. McManus, general manager of the Hearst-Selig News Pictorial service, said, "The one striking new feature of modern life is the wider and wider diffusion of information. The press hitherto has been a great instrument of this beneficent work. With the supreme inventive genius of modern men the press has been supplemented by the moving picture, which not only gives the same wide presentation of the subject, but which visualizes it in presenting it pictorially, and which has established itself a new and vital educational force in the modern civilized community." The party then proceeded to Filmland on the Zone, the Exposition's entertainment area, where a beauty contest was in progress. Twenty-five aspirants posed for the camera. The evening was completed when Art Smith, The Bird Boy of Fort Wayne, mounted his illuminated aeroplane and, in the still evening sky, climbed to 3,000 feet only then to descend in a crazed looping spiral corkscrewing dive with the fusees on his wing sparking and flashing as if indicating the foreshadowing of a fiery and fatal crash. Thousands below watched in amazement. Thousands more watched from San Francisco's surrounding hills. But all witnessed finally a carefully designed but thrilling aerobatic stunt. When safely on the ground, Smith was presented with a gold medal by Francis X. Bushman, the head of Metro Pictures. The presentation was not filmed. Later, the negative plates were developed. The overexposed still photography record of his recent flight, that seemingly aborted night flight, was developed. The message in the madness could finally be read. There, in a cursively connected script of flare and fire, was the salutation, M E T R O, etched in bright white light into the black night, enveloping the whole wide San Francisco Bay and the cities and towns on its shores and even in the hills and valleys beyond.

It is said that in one year when the population of the United States was 90 million, 17 million saw Lincoln Beachey, The Man Who Owns the Sky, fly. A San Franciscan, Lincoln Beachey, The Master Birdman, was the obvious first choice to be the featured stunt aviator at the 1915 Panama-Pacific International Exposition. He opened the fair with an amazing feat, taking off inside the Machinery Palace on the exposition grounds, flying his Curtiss Pusher at 60 miles per hour, and landing it, all within the confines of the hall. Art Smith, The Bird Boy of Fort Wayne, assisted Beachey's performances, an understudy of sorts, who in his midget race car would chase the low flying master along the Avenue of the Palms. On March 14th, Beachey launched out over the Bay in his new monoplane to perform his famous maneuver, a series of inside loops. But the overpowered airplane's controls could not handle the torque and the strain. The plane crumpled and fell into the water between two Navy ships. He survived the crash, the autopsy later revealed, but was unable to escape the harness. He drowned. Art Smith took his place, flying the daily demonstrations and the nightly skywriting shows spotlit by the

General Electric Scintillator emanating from the Tower of Jewels. But before that, he needed to practice, to attempt to reach the skill of his recently deceased mentor and friend, Lincoln Beachey. "An aeroplane in the hands of Lincoln Beachey," Orville Wright had said, "was poetry." Smith needed a place to learn to write in the sky. He needed a place, too, to steady the nerves, tamp down the tide of rising fears, to be alone with his machine in the air and the dynamic physics of not falling even as you fall. He discovered, twenty miles south of San Francisco, the necropolis of Colma, California. Colma, the city of cemeteries. After the earthquake, the city of San Francisco had closed the cemeteries in the city and evicted the dead. Beachey had been buried somewhere down there. The fields were a patchwork of tombs, mausoleums, ossuaries. Art Smith bombed the fields with flowers. Then with the wings of his aeroplane outfitted with small smudge pots, railroad flares, roman candles, Art Smith wrote for the dead. Again and again, he wrote, writing, always beginning in a profound dive, mimicking an out-of-control tailspin to make his gyrations look erratic, but, in reality, he was spelling out, in the exhaust, little prayers, letter to letter to letter, each ligature a bridge, a reprieve, each serif another breath caught and another, a stair-stepping signature. He wanted to feel the weightlessness as he fell, sense the levitation of the smoke as it rose up behind him and was propelled upward by the rising heat of the highlands below. Somewhere down there was what was left of Beachey and up above were the streamers of smoke, the trail of sparks, braiding together like wraiths, like ghosts, like stars, the rising residue of *colmacolmacolma*.

Terre Haute

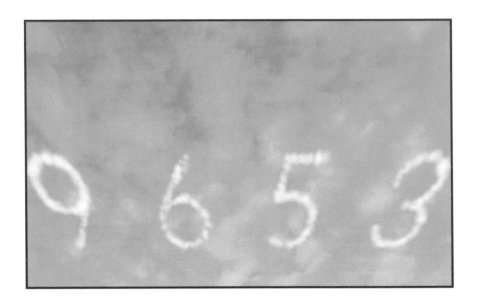

On Christmas, 1921, President Warren G. Harding commuted the sentence of Socialist Eugene V. Debs who had been imprisoned since 1919 in Atlanta for sedition. Debs arrived home in Terre Haute, Indiana, three days later and was met at the rail depot by thousands of cheering Terre Hauteans. At that moment, Art Smith, The Bird Boy of Fort Wayne, was aloft, over the city known as The Crossroads of America, the intersection of highways 40 and 41, affixing the number 9 6 5 3 in frigid pristine Indiana air. This is not an estimate of attendance or of the crowd size gathered on the ground, but the number given to the famous agitator and pacifist (now speaking animatedly from the open vestibule platform of the observation car below) by the Federal Bureau of Prisons. As Convict #9653, Debs had run for President of the United States, again, his fifth attempt, the year before, garnering nearly a million votes while behind bars. Art Smith had heard of Debs, but had not voted for him. In fact, there appears to be no record of his having voted for anyone at all. He had been and would be in the future on the move, never establishing a permanent residence really. And, as he was often perched high overhead, flying over precincts and wards, more often than not, he felt detached from the earthbound goings on beneath him. Even though he allowed the epithet of "The Bird Boy of Fort Wayne" to remain connected to his name, trailing Art Smith like the new advertising banners he had begun to deploy behind his aircraft to augment his skywriting, he no longer felt attached to that place as he once did. A Bird Boy, yes, but of Fort Wayne, less and less. Politics and the voting that accompanied it, he understood, was attached to place. No, it had dawned on him a while ago that he was now, more and more, a citizen of the sky. Debs had been sentenced to ten years hard labor, and he had been disenfranchised for life for his seditious speech at Canton, Ohio, during the Great War. In many ways, Debs too was as disconnected from the world as Smith was now. Even bound he had been unbound, not local but global. Rootless.

The Root Glass Company had originally lured Art Smith to The Crossroads of America. In 1915, the company entered a contest to design and exclusively manufacture a new proprietary bottle for the Coca-Cola Company. Their design, inspired by the ribbed and ellipsoid contour of the cocoa plant seedpod, shown here,

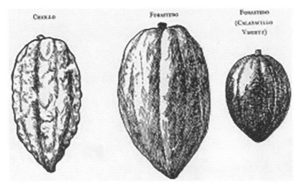

won the competition handily and their "hobble-skirt" bottle, cast in the distinctive German Green glass, was an instant success, and the container remains connected to what it contains even today a century later. In 1921, the patent for the product was about to expire. Coca-Cola and Root embarked on a campaign, the first of its kind, to have not just the name or slogan or text about a product trademarked but also its actual package. Its vessel would speak the protected name. A shape would be a brand. To that end the companies hired a semi-ridged dirigible, similar to the one shown here,

One of the U. S. Navy Observation Balloons in flight.

to hover over The Crossroads of America and, through an act of subliminal free association, have the public below connect the shape of the blimp to the bottle to the seedpod to the product. Art Smith contributed to the effort circling the oblong balloon and skywriting the company's name in such a manner as its oblong O's seemed to effervesce, floating, making a halo of haloes around the airship.

The skies over Terre Haute, The Crossroads of America, bustled in the closing days of 1921. Eugene V. Debs had been released from prison and been welcomed home a hero. The Root Glass Company had captured lightning in a bottle and the bottle itself had become a kind of lightning. Hulman & Company also was headquartered in Terre Haute, a wholesale grocery and manufactory of leavening agents. Now as the company wished to expand into the retail market, they considered a rebranding as well. Art Smith experimented with his new idea of a more permanent form of "skywriting." He would write his message in bold letters printed on giant panels of silk. The message? The chemical formula for the company's signature product, baking soda. The streaming silk banner unfurling and flapping in Art Smith's wake dictated that he create, in the face of the banner's new and unique aerodynamics, whole new techniques and tweaks for steering and stirring the aircraft for sustaining controlled flight. The buffeting was an amplification of the popping and puckering of the scarf he wore around his neck that would slap him, wrapping around his head and blinding him during gravitational gyrations caused by his acrobatic maneuverings. The tail of letters had a life of its own in the slipstream. But flying with a banner was in no way as challenging as the actual production of letters out of thin air. He easily set his stick and throttle to a kind of automatic course, a slow broad circle over The Crossroads of America with the actual crossroads below serving as a kind of center on which he pivoted. It wasn't challenging to fly this way simply hauling the letters, letters that seemed nonsensical to him, lugging them through the lower thicker air. And he could continue to display the advertisement even into clouds, clots that rose into lofts of white wispy loafs, that accumulated and expanded into billowing banks and bluffs in which he would disappear only to reappear, his trailing message intact like a ticker tape threading itself through gloved fingers. There was that. He didn't need an empty sky to promote this leavening agent. Hulman & Company would rename the baking soda Clabber Girl in the New Year. And he would be back with another banner calibrated to the new name, churning and chugging through an undulating cloudscape, a curdled buttermilk sky.

Ohio

A year before his own death, Art Smith, found himself in western Ohio at the service of First National Pictures, advertising with his skywriting the company's new moving picture, *The Lost World*. His mission brought him over the Little Miami River valley to The Land of the Cross-Tipped Churches, a farming region settled by immigrant German Catholics who still spoke a Westphalian, Oldenburgian, and Lower Saxonic dialect, an isogloss, centered around the Grand Lake St. Mary. Minster, Fort Loramie, St. Rose, Montezuma, St. Henry, Sebastian, Cassella, Chickasaw, and Maria Stein, all these towns featured 19th-century red brick Gothic Catholic churches with their steeples topped with crosses. Art Smith could navigate the valley by means of steeple, using the spires as a kind of slalom pylon, banking, vectoring back and forth over the rich grid of quilted farmland spread out between the towns. He was flying a new WACO 7 biplane, shaking down the prototype for the Advance Aircraft Company, the manufacturer, headquartered just a few miles north in Troy. *The Lost World*, a silent movie, was adapted from a book written by Arthur Conan Doyle who appeared in the front piece of the film as himself, introducing the trailing adventure. The movie concerned a scientific expedition to a lost and forgotten plateau in Venezuela of intimidating geology, ancient flora, and prehistoric beasts, dinosaurs of all kinds. Smith had been told by the accounts office at First Republic that Doyle himself, without revealing the source as a Hollywood movie, had taken test reels showing the various dinosaurs fighting and grazing and flying to a meeting of the Society of American Magicians. The audience, which included Houdini, was astonished by the extraordinary lifelike visuals concocted by the trick photography. The stop-action animation effects were created by Willis O'Brien who years later would place an articulated puppet, King Kong, on a model Empire State Building attacked by a swarm of live split-screen projected Naval Reserve Curtiss O2C-2 biplanes. Art Smith would not live to see that monster's death, but now he sat stone still, amazed in the darkened theater in Celina, Ohio, by the sight of the rampaging allosaurus attacking a family of terrified triceratops. He could, if he thought about it and if he looked very closely, see the slight twitch in the joints and limbs of the models as they moved, skipping from one frame of film to the next, but it was mostly seamless, this illusion of movement, how the eyes and the brain smoothed things over in the dark, skipping stone to stone, like his plane's invisible ligature from one inanimate and monstrous letter to the next until it made sense.

Art Smith thought that, from a distance, the holey, moth-eaten exhaust-ed strokes of his message looked a lot like the slivers of bone, splinters of wood, shards of marble, threads of fabric, locks of hair, or crumbs of cartilage on display at The Shrine of the Holy Relics in the town of Maria Stein. He had a whole week in The Land of the Cross-Tipped Churches, writing each day on the erased and refreshed vault of heaven overhead, a rosary of quirky quickly decaying letters commanding the *volk* below to attend this strange new movie. By the time he landed his WACO in a pasture or gleaned field—this was northwestern Ohio after all, full of flatness, that had been, at one time, the vast flat floor to an ancient inland sea after having been scraped flat by an eon of sanding by tidal waves of ice age glaciers—to visit the towns he daily flew over, he could regard his melting handiwork, gauge the remnants of his writing in the sky, now shattered fragments, scratches, smears. On one such landing he poked his head into The Shrine with its colorful and ornately carved side altars and reliquaries. Several Sisters of the Most Precious Blood knelt in a continuous vigil of veneration, murmuring prayers toward a forest of host-encumbered monstrances and ostensoria. There were the displayed relics but also everywhere else, in the aisles and the alcoves, there were cartons and crates of relics, shipped to The Shrine for safety as the Great War in Europe bloomed and churches there were consumed in the bombardments and conflagrations. Now, in 1925, there were no churches to return the bones to and The Shrine was becoming a parody of archeology, buried in artifacts with no spoil at all.

After finishing that day's application of L O S T W O R L D, Art Smith glided smoothly downward, landing in a vast field outside of the town of Maria Stein that he soon discovered was the test track for the New Idea agricultural implement factory. As he descended, Smith saw several teams hauling the New Idea manure spreaders, their ground driven gears and axles rotating the flails and paddles at the rear of the wagons that launched the chaff of agitated chopped manure and broadcast it in wide arches in their wakes. He landed into the wind, of course, and through the layers of rich ripe and ripening smells, skipping over the slick, wet treated furrows below and jinking around and over the lifting roiled columns of steaming clouds of dust to find solid ground off in a far corner of the field. On the ground he looked back over to where the machines were working, the dung eruptions' acrobatic percolations, amused by this other kind of terrestrial "writing" spewing from another tail end. The "new idea" had been another use for the wing, the winglike paddles set at odd angles that aerated, scooped, and threw the wide-ranging shit.

The first prehistoric beast seen by the explorers in the movie *The Lost World* is the flying reptile pteranodon. Art Smith, The Bird Boy of Fort Wayne, on the last day of skywriting advertisements for the film above the villages of western Ohio spelled out the name (from the Greek for toothless wing) of the soaring dinosaur. The pteranodon circles above the Venezuelan plateau of The Lost World, working the invisible thermals, Smith knew, with its voluminous ribbed wings spanning over twenty feet, half the length of wingspan of his own WACO 7. Its sleek head looked like a missile, the long sharpened beak blending back into the narrow skull topped with tapering dorsal crest of some kind, like the vertical rudder on a plane. How strange it all was. Smith concentrated on the spelling. He had made several mistaken efforts already. The fourth and final effort is shown here. The name was strange. Foreign. From another world itself. All vowels and a bizarre unknown digraph. And what was stranger, Smith asked himself, the haunting image captured on film or knowing that the articulated model of the beast represented a long lost reality of the fossil record? The pteranodon

had once soared using the same convection and physics that were second nature to him in the air over Ohio.

Later that year, *The Lost World* would become the first movie to be shown to passengers on a regularly scheduled airliner. Imperial Airways, flying from London to Paris, presented the nine passengers on a Handley-Page O/400 the fantasy film of forgotten time. The plane, a converted bomber constructed of canvas and wood, was a dangerous setting to show the movie with its highly flammable nitrate film stock. A few months before, Art Smith, leaving The Land of Cross-Tipped Churches, devised one last signature to affix above the Maumee River Valley, the M O V E being torpedoed by a dive-bombing "i." The print of *The Lost World*, having been a hit with its multiple showings in Celina, was now being transported by another WACO plane, the brand new WACO 8, the company's first cabin craft, a big biplane seating six, to Toledo, the big city to the north on Lake Erie. Art Smith, The Bird Boy, escorted the ungainly 8 in its early evening departure, having already inscribed his cryptic farewell to the towns below. Later that year, upon hearing of the news from Europe that they had shown *The Lost World* movie in a moving airplane, he remembered his own flight that night, starboard and slightly trailing the bumbling big transport as it made its jerking lurches and inarticulate stuttering stalls to altitude. He remembered the flickering of illumination, the flashes of light he caught sight of through the big cabin windows of the 8 and the dark silhouettes inside, transfixed, staring dead ahead, spellbound, lost.

French Lick

In 1917, the bottler of Pluto Water, the trademark of the natural mineral spring sourced in French Lick, Indiana, needed over 450 boxcars to ship that year's output to America. The water, naturally carbonated and salted with sodium and magnesium sulfate, was a very popular product, strongly laxative. The prehistoric spring had been tapped by humans for a long time and was always regarded as medicinal and restorative. That year, Art Smith, The Bird Boy of Fort Wayne, was commissioned by former U.S. Senator Thomas Taggart, owner of the grand resort, The French Lick Springs Hotel, to affix "America's Laxative," Pluto Water's other motto, "When Nature Won't Pluto Will," over the pristine karst region that generated the refreshing cure. It took a long time to construct the slogan above the resort, and its articulation could be read as well by the clients situated in rocking chairs and chaise longues on the grand portico of the other deluxe hotel rival at nearby West Baden Springs. Pluto Water's published advertisement guaranteed effective relief within a half-hour to two hours after ingestion. And it did take Art Smith the better part of the morning to complete the task, the zigzagging double-ues being particularly tricky. Pluto Water remained profitable for many years after, growing in popularity until the operation was shuttered in the seventies when lithium, which was found in trace amounts in the water, was deemed a controlled substance by the federal government and hence no longer legal to purvey.

That same year, on a Tuesday, in 1917, world famous chef, Louis Perrin, began to prepare breakfast for the guests of the French Lick Springs Hotel only to discover the kitchen had run out of orange juice and oranges to create more. Improvising, he began to squeeze tomatoes, of which he had bushels, combining the acidic juice with sugar and his special sauce that, to this day, remains secret, and served the new drink in the resort's dining rooms. The concoction was an instant success, and its fame quickly spread by means of departing conventioneers, spa vacationers, and the gambling gangsters and bootleggers who would park their private rail parlor cars on special sidings at the front door of the hotel. Management had extended Art Smith's skywriting contract, and, after a heated discussion with Chef Perrin on what to call the new beverage, settled on what was then a startling appellation—Tomato Juice. It is interesting to think that Art Smith was there at the moment of inception for so many innovations and inventions. And just as interesting, no one at the time, at those times, knew how it would all turn out, how things would unfold, how history would express itself at long last. And Art Smith, it seemed, would be there to mark so many of these occasions with his skywriting even though that writing was not indelible and the content of each message soon forgotten whilst the grandness and surprise of the gesture would remain fixed only in the consciousness of the witnesses of each temporary, transitory display. Art took to the air, creating a kind of a palimpsest of smoke and vapor, overwriting that day's tribute to Pluto Water in the sky above the tiny village of French Lick, now barely remembered as the original source of these two important digestive aperitifs.

Good
Night

From late March to December 4th of 1915, Art Smith, The Bird Boy of Fort Wayne, closed the day's festivities at the Panama-Pacific International Exposition in San Francisco with an inspiring display of aerial acrobatics. It was in those night performances over the brightly illuminated fair grounds that the "skywriting" he invented transcended even the transcendent miracle of simple unannotated flight. A dozen years after Kill Devil Hill, at the dawn of the aviation era, the fairgoers on the ground were still startled when the air above them became crowded with these new winged machines. And then this, Art Smith, The Bird Boy, with his darting back and forth, rustles the abstract clouds together, into these floating advertisements of their own wonder. Each night, Art Smith would construct out of thin air, it seemed, first the word G O O D that, more often than not, was misread as G O D, invisible in the dark, the persistent hum and the changing pitch as the letters bloomed. By the end of the Exposition's run, Smith said he could create the words with his eyes closed, string them together in his sleep as if they were a notation of a dream.

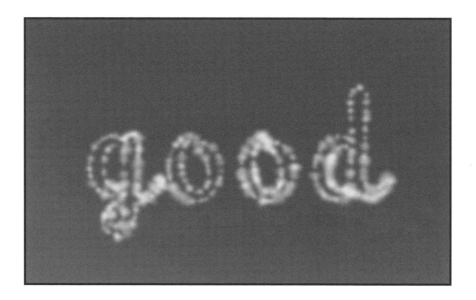

That last night, that last G O O D N I G H T, floating in the sky over the Bay, Smith opened his eyes to see the hundreds of spotlights of the fair below blink out one by one, the search lights, too, that lit the Tower of Jewels and all the jewels that refracted and reflected the light flickered and went dark, the light bathing the halls and palaces damped and smothered, the strings of lights outlining the turrets and funnels and masts of the battleships and cruisers below him went black, the ships sank into darkness. With every other source of light extinguished, snuffed out, the word N I G H T itself alone, arching over the blackout city below, seemed to retain its own internal phosphorescence, a cooling ember as it dimmed. Maybe it was a mirage of some kind, an afterimage on the back of his eyelids. Everyone's eyes had been changed by the Exposition. Not just what they had seen but how now they would see. Even in the now black black night, N I G H T lingered. Art Smith flew back over the cloud-shrouded mountain range of letters, looking for the "i" to dot—a swoop, a scallop, a wing. And then he flew out into the endless darkness of the opaque Pacific.

Acknowledgments

Airplane Reading: "J n 2 T m A R r e D," "W H E N";

Always Crashing: "B O O M," "x";

American Short Fiction: "A M A N";

Bennington Review: "BENDAY," "L U C K Y," "N O T H I N G";

Big Other: "French Lick";

Brooklyn Rail: "i f," "w r I g h t";

The Collagist: "!!!!";

Economy: "m a y d a y";

Gargoyle: "B I R T H," "GOOD NIGHT," "M E T R O";

Ghost Town: "WordCross";

Golden Handcuffs Review: "G O";

Guest House: "m o o n," "R E S T," "t h i n," "SPIRAL";

Iowa Review: "E," "W O W O";

Literari Quarterly: "R A I S E";

Ocean State: "l a r k";

Passages North: "T H E S U N," "leadlead," "Blimp";

Pleiades: "s c a l e";

Postcard Press: "AIM ME";

Prompt Press: "S T I L L";

Salt Hill: "HELL";

Seneca Review: "string";

Split Lip: "SIGHT";

Story: "LOST";

Tammy: "A B C";

Thin Air: "M O M," "W O W";

Unstuck: "&";

Upstreet: "F L E W," "Star dusting," "i c e d";
Waxwing: "9653";
Western Humanities Review: "A Ai," "ART" "CLOUD," "l o o l."

Rachel Sherwood Roberts's book *Art Smith: Pioneer Aviator*, published by McFarland & Company in 2003, was the wind beneath my wings. Thank you for this history even more unbelievable than my small fictions.

Wingman: Brian Oliu, the severely clear visuals are all his. Twelve o'clock high and higher.

Altimeter; Compass; Attitude, Heading, Turn, Airspeed Indicators at Squadron BOA.

An Alabama Murmuration: Robin Behn, Wendy Rawlings, Joel Brouwer, Kellie Wells, Heidi Lynn Staples, Hali Felt, L. Lamar Wilson, John Estes, Fred Whiting, Deborah Weiss, Heather White, Emily Wittman, Yolanda Manora, Albert Pionke, William Ulmer, Patti White, Karen Gardiner, Nathan Parker, Tasha Coryell, Kevin Waltman, Jessica Kidd, Eric Parker, Trudier Harris, Phil Beidler, John Crowley, Bruce Smith, Joyelle McSweeney, Kate Bernheimer, Lex Williford, Dave Madden, Peter Streckfus, Lucy Pickering, Andy Johnson, Michael Meija and Mindy Wilson, Kathy Merrell, Bill and Bebe Barefoot Lloyd, Leslie and Dan Hogue, Grace Aberdean, Jason McCall, Jeremy Butler, Frannie James, Melissa Delbridge, Charles Morgan, and Sandy Huss.

"Thank you, Sioux City. See you on the ground": Joe Geha and Fern Kupfer, Steve Pett and Clare Cardinal, Sam Pritchard and Tista Simpson, Susan Carlson, Rosanne Potter, David Hamilton, Kathy Hall, Mary Swander, Anne Hunsinger, Jane Dupuis, Rick Moody, and Laurel Nakadate.

Flight Instruction. Instrument Certification: John Barth, Scott Sanders, Edmund White, Dana Wichern, David Hamilton, Howard Junker.

Finger Four Formation: Tessa Fontaine, Jess Richardson, Betsy Seymour, Dara Ewing.

The Tuscaloosa Pursuit Squadron: Jim Merrell, Hobson Bryan, David Allgood, Sam Rombokas, Bob Lyman, Mirza Beg, Jim Labauve, Steve Davis, Bill Buchanan, Lee Pike, Dan Waterman.

En Route Air Traffic Control: Rachel Yoder, Jenny Colville, Jennie ver Steeg, Colin Rafferty, Elizabeth Wade, Jennifer Gravley, Matt Dube, Miles and Susan Gibson (Spitfire and Hurricane), Michael Czyzniejewski and Karen Craigo, Del Lausa, Vivian Dorsel, Lauren Leja, Alicia Mathais, Greg Hauser, Nik De Dominic, Cindi Speros Yonts, Sejal Shah, Chris Riley, and Mark Feldman.

Indiana Migratory Flyways: Julia Meek, Dawn Burns, Linda Oblack, Sarah Jacobi, Dan Zweig, Jill Christman, Mark Neely, Jean Kane, Patty Brotherson, Kathy Curtis, Linda Dibblee, Irene and Robert Walters, Wayne, Ruth and Andrew Payne.

Dead Stick Landers and Controlled Crashes: Sean Loveless and Peggy Shinner.

Approaches, Departures: Marian Young.

Wing Warpers, Wing Walkers: Susan Neville, Michael Rosen, Jay Brandon, Michael Wilkerson, Ann Jones, Nancy Esposito, Rikki Ducornet, Valerie Miner, Melanie Rae Thon, Louise Erdrich, Paul Maliszewski.

Airbase Martone: Tim, Amy, Ben, and Gina.

Lift, Drag, Weight, Thrust: Sam and Nick.

Pitch, Yaw, Roll, and Center of Gravity: Theresa.

About the Author

Michael Martone was born in Fort Wayne, Indiana, where he learned at a very early age about flight. His mother, a high school English teacher, read to him of the adventures of Daedalus and Icarus from the book *Mythology* written by Edith Hamilton, who was born in Dresden, Germany, but who also grew up in Fort Wayne, Indiana. Martone remembers being taken by his father to Baer Field, the commercial airport and Air National Guard base, to watch the air traffic there. He was blown backward on the observation deck by the prop-wash of the four-engine, aluminum-skinned Lockheed Constellation with its elegant three-tailed rudder turning away from the gates. At the same time, the jungle-camouflaged Phantom F-4s did touch-and-goes on the long runway, the ignition of their after-burners sounding as if the sky was being torn like blue silk. As a child growing up in Fort Wayne, Indiana, Martone heard many stories about Art Smith, "The Bird Boy of Fort Wayne," and the adventures of this early aviation pioneer. In the air above the city, Martone, as a boy, imagined, "The Bird Boy of Fort Wayne" accomplishing, for the first time, the nearly impossible outside loop and then a barrel-roll back into a loop-to-loop in his fragile cotton canvas and baling wire flying machine he built in his own backyard in Fort Wayne, Indiana, whose sky above was the first sky, anywhere, to be written on, written on by Art Smith, "The Bird Boy of Fort Wayne," the letters hanging there long enough to be read but then smeared, erased by the high altitude wind, turning into a dissipating front of fogged memories, cloudy recollection.

BOA Editions, Ltd.
American Reader Series

Colophon

BOA Editions, Ltd., a not-for-profit publisher of poetry and other literary works, fosters readership and appreciation of contemporary literature. By identifying, cultivating, and publishing both new and established poets and selecting authors of unique literary talent, BOA brings high-quality literature to the public. Support for this effort comes from the sale of its publications, grant funding, and private donations.

The publication of this book is made possible, in part, by the special support of the following individuals:

Anonymous
David Fraher, *in memory of A. Poulin, Jr.*
James Long Hale
Art & Pam Hatton
Sandi Henschel, *in memory of Anthony Piccione*
Joe McElveney
Dorrie Parini & Paul LaFerriere
Boo Poulin
Steven O. Russell & Phyllis Rifkin-Russell
Sejal Shah & Rajesh Singaravelu, *in honor of Marjorie B. Searl*
Allan & Melanie Ulrich
William Waddell & Linda Rubel